Degenerative Prose:
Writing Beyond Category

EDITED BY MARK AMERIKA AND RONALD SUKENICK

Published by FC2 with support given by the Unit for Contemporary Literature of Illinois State University, the Illinois Arts Council, and the Arts and Humanities Assembly of Boulder/Neodata Endowment for the Arts and Humanities.

Photo credits: Sante D' Dorazio, American Photo, Jan/Feb 94: Vol. 5, #1 (page 91); Richard Young/Rex USA, People Weekly, Sept 20 1993 (page 98).

The Anarchivist of Eco-Dub, a screen-based Acrobatic Hyperfiction, appears courtesy of Alternative-X, an electronic publishing network found on the world-wide-web (http://www.altx.com).

Degenerative Prose: Writing Beyond Category
Edited by Mark Amerika and Ronald Sukenick

ISBN: 1-57366-008-6   Paper, US$9.00

Produced and printed in the United States of America.

Book Design: Michael Shernick
Cover Art: Rikki Ducornet

Acknowledgements

The editors wish to thank all the editors, writers, artists, designers, production assistants, students, sponsors, and dedicated readers who, over the years, have made *Black Ice* magazine's existence possible.

This book was originally published as a special 10th anniversary double issue of *Black Ice* magazine (numbers 11 & 12). As with all *Black Ice* material, the writing herein is treacherous and dangerous to your health.

Degenerative Prose: A Virtual Intro

MARK AMERIKA AND RON SUKENICK

To: sukenick@spot.colorado.edu
From: amerika@altx.com
Subject: Degenerative Prose: A Virtual Intro
Bcc:
X-Attachments:

Hi Ron,

I guess this is our intro. My name is Mark Amerika. I am an addict.
An addict of Degenerative Prose. Of anything that re-synthesizes
wild, hybridized forms of prose including fiction, faction, friction
and non-diction.

What I'm wondering is this: how can we collate all the really cool
stuff we keep getting sent to us for Black Ice magazine and turn it
into the next hip marketing concept? Something like Degenerative
Prose. Or how about Degenerative Pose? De-Gen-X Poseur?

Mark

_____

From: sukenick@spot.Colorado.edu
To: amerika@altx.com
Subject: Degenerative Prose: A Virtual Intro
Bcc:
X-Attachments:

Dear marketing amerika—i don't like the idea of turning ideas into
marketing concepts however much we may bullshit about this—
degenerative prose was simply a way of describing the inter- or non-
generic prose we picked for this issue of Black Ice—it's a way of
talking about what appears to be a new synthesis that seems on the
verge of crystallizing: degenerative: inter-genre, generation (of new
realities), prose of a new generation, destruction of stale genres,

1

proud assumption of insult & injury hurled by p.c. left and radical right against anything that violates their narrow sense of morality, our sense of the need to transgress the latter in form and content: THEREBY: providing ways for fiction to INTERVENE in, rather than merely add to (as in Surfiction,) or worse, imitate (as in "Realism") reality, however you define the latter. Thus DEGENERATIVE PROSE is a vehicle for the new style of INTERVENTIVE FICTION, which is not so much fiction as narrative, there being important differences. I hope this answers all your questions and solves all your problems. rONsUK.

---

to: sukenick@spot.colorado.edu
from: amerika@altx.com
Subject: Degenerative Prose: A Virtual Intro
Bcc:
X-Attachments:

R(ight)ON!

I like your line:

DEGENERATIVE PROSE is a vehicle for the new style of INTERVENTIVE FICTION, which is not so much fiction as narrative, there being important differences.

absolutely. interventive narratives subvert the mainstream impulse to exclude radical discourse in favor of hopeless banalities. but we need to work hard and fight for a more freely-accessed distributed environment where associative headless groups of artists can cultivate home-grown networks whose capacity to expand is greater than ever before. for the ultimate impact on the mainstream host's rapidly decomposing body, we need to first inter-link, then inter-vene. we can't be afraid of the chaos (and become christian fundamentalists), instead, we need to *become* the chaos, *use* the chaos to inter-vene and decompose the rise of christian fundamentalism. inter-net is making this all the more con-vene-ient.

also, as you say, this is about inter-generational demystification of genre-styled writing: sci-fi, boob-tube, sex-kitten, magical historical hyperrealism et al, ATE it all, digested it, then found out there was more here than meets the I. first of all, demagnify the ego and

2

crank up the id. then turn on the eros-machine and see what all else melts in its Wake.

degenerative prose destabilizes the once-monumental, elitist Narrative Zone. finished again, we (of the *degenerative network*) finally begin to create an intricate web of wander-lusting particles that can launch themselves OUT into the big space, the big space of IN. in this seamless net of hypertextual activity, an interview becomes a manifesto becomes a performance becomes a press release becomes a cult object known for its radical subjectivity.

I just realized what I mean by radical subjectivity: what I'm talking about is creating a sound-effect. computers don't create sound-effects. they are tools that *artists* use to create sound-effects. now who's to say what sounds have what effects and how do visual properties like words on a page create the kind of *necessary* sound-effect one needs in order to live through the day?

with all this noise being cranked up especially for our distraction (see O.J., see Newt, see Rush, see the battle over PBS & the NEA),the idea of *editorial vision* will become more relevant than ever.

that's where we come in. the degenerative prose editors, the virtual filtering system that takes the chaotic electrosphere for what it is and reorganizes it in such a way as to create

_____. Please fill in the blank.

alt-x

_____

to: amerika@altx.com
from: sukenick@spot.colorado.edu
Subject: Degenerative Prose: A Virtual Intro
Bcc:
X-Attachments:

i'm not sure what you mean by sound effects, unless effects that are sound, which i'm all for. nor why you're so worried about funnymentalist christians, who are only troublesome insofar as the conglomerate culture decides to make room for them. the same can be said of us subterraneans, by the way. in the praxis of everyday life, money is gravity and only magicians and shamans have anti-gravity capability.

maybe such types know how to use what you call radical subjectivity, but it's certain that only those with anti-gravity capability can intervene in conglomerate culture and interrupt its relentless flow toward media-ocrity, negativity and the kind of destruction that always happens when those with nazi dreams are unleashed. that happens when the healthy forces of chaos, which stir the creative pot, give way to the 2nH=BB]=F76Mo=D9=B3=FB=F7=B3gk=A8/7+=B5=E6=ED=FB=F7=B1=E5=B7=C4=F7=CDo=FB=BBN)Jx=D2=FOexactly (must have been something i had for lunch)—anyway, you know the diff between chaos which seethes with possibility, and turbulence or pure nose which is just down the drain—so the idea is not to give way to the latter—so though we are but maggots digesting the wastes and rottenness of the conglomerate body, we have at least that transformational talent—to degenerate and generate—and go from there in the electrosphere—over and out

---

to: sukenick@spot.colorado.edu
from: amerika@altx.com
Subject: Degenerative Prose: A Virtual Intro
Bcc:
X-Attachments:

down & in,

would you say that for those of us subterraneans who get lost in the praxis of everyday life, money itself becomes anti-gravity and this in turn causes us to realize that the only magicians and shamans who can remain grounded are the ones who know how to use what you call radical subjectivity? i guess it's a guarantee that only those who are grounded can intervene in conglomerate culture and interrupt its relentless flow toward idiocy, banality, pseudo-positivism and the kind of destruction that always happens when the monsters of Reason are unleashed.

but is chaos really healthy? are the forces of chaos, the degenerative prose artists lost in a dysfunctionally narrativized mist, and who stir the creative pot and give way to the overdetermined morass of

"n H = B B] = F 7 6 M o = D 9 = B 3 = F B = F 7 = B 3 g k = A 8 /
7+=B5=E6=ED=FB=F7=B1=E5=B7=C4=F7=CDo=FB=BBN)]x=D2=FOexactly",
what they appear to be? or have they forgotten that even Avant-
Pop Will Eat Itself? (we just went out back and checked the organic
compost heap—very steamy and the worms are not only still alive
and multiplying, the shit is getting richer! the closer you get to the
center the hotter it gets. you are where you came from hence?)

as you say, there *is* a diff between chaos which seethes with possibility, and turbulence (one is pure schnoz, the other is just more
noise swirling around the brain of the programming-agent)—it
makes me wonder if the space of present time isn't too dimensional
and what kind of emergency broadcast network we need to launch
in order to stir the embers? Is it Time yet? Como? Fuerte you cum?
(Regarding lunch & what you ate—tums).

the sound effects I was talking about have to do with acoustical
space and how every image, word and vibration that tries to influence how & what we think is somehow connected to the regenera-
tive tissues of a despotic numbed musculature that tries to bring us
down to earth—a cellular level—one that we can take flight from
by entering the big space, the big space of IN. INNER SPACE/
OUTER HOUSE. building a virtual shit-castle to get lost in.

I believe we can best experience these effects through music, which
somehow reminds me of Joyce, how he wasn't missing a beat, and
how now they pass laws that limit the amounts of beat per minute
you can play before they arrest you (because the music itself arrests
them and they don't think it's very funnymennalist at all!), wait,
Here Comes Everybody, there's some wild, trippy, degenerative drug
being passed around (in paper sacks it looks like), a work-in-progress,
the acclammitation of all of those narratives, ONE EXACTLY, endless short story, the Grammatron writing-machine translating your
experience *for* you *as* you experience it, developmental software program blissed out on a dangerous combination of digital dis-
tortions now permeating the electrosphere...

up in the blood

———————

to: amerika@altx.com
from: sukenick@spot.colorado.edu

Subject: Degenerative Prose: A Virtual Intro
Bcc:
X-Attachments:

up & in,

no, i insist, money is the gravity of our culture and it's not all bad. i like money, don't you? but there is a counterforce and the counterforce is groovity. where gravity is heavy groovity is light. where gravity is day groovity is night. about midnight. where gravity plods groovity dances. where gravity feeds your stomach groovity feeds your mind. where gravity is power groovity is joy. and like that.

as far as the monsters of reason go, they of course are the results of gravity, gravity leads to depravity. but what can groovity not lead to? maybe the monsters of unreason are worse than the monsters of reason—or maybe they come to the same thing. us is sometimes worse than them, i have seen it. don't forget hitler was an artist—and a vegetarian—a real new ager in fact, really into psychic phenomena, only drank mint tea, THE WHOLE BIT. Goering was an esthete, a bigtime artlover. real groovy. this is exactly why Avant-Pop has to eat itself, turn itself into fertilizer before it gets turned into bullshit—Avant-Poop. Avant-Plop. Avant-Flop.

i like acoustic space because it provides a bridge from inner space to the outside since it functions in both. but i never did like staying inside. i need to get out there and intervene, permeate, as you typocoin, with the electrosphere, translating, as you say, my experience as i go—but translating it into what, come to think—maybe translating it into think. so how about it, do you think to come or do you come to think?

down & imp

---

to: sukenick@spot.colorado.edu
from: amerika@altx.com
Subject: Degenerative Prose: A Virtual Intro
Bcc:
X-Attachments:

down and imp,

you're really getting into the groovity of things. you must be rolling in the dough or doling out the roe. eggs-ackly. belly of sunshine withdraws into alkaline speed recovery and then what have you got? guerrillas in the midst: hungering for the kill.

these hitlerian new age mutant ninja hackers are eggs-ackly what i'm talking about. let them eat laptops. suck on the hyper-hip wetdream of bodily obsolescence. why not? the great all-giving Morph God has one goal in mind and that is packaged revolution. or co-evolution: the stratification of the spheres. holy-go-lightly (down into the pit of reason where imaginative discourse starves for ideas...but not marketing concepts...or are these digestive tracts we keep circulating in the electrosphere riding on the wings of those necessary angels whose job it is to take us up into the big space of IN? what do we do when we get there?)

come to think of it maybe the enzyme that cums internally is the one that fuels our come-as-it-may thought-process. but this is alimentary, isn't it Professore?

Domain Name Unknown

---

to: amerika@altx.com
from: sukenick@spot.colorado.edu
Subject: Degenerative Prose: A Virtual Intro
Bcc:
X-Attachments:

Rabble to babble: as i was saying—what are we talking about and do we know?—do we need to know?—strikes me what we're into is a little electronic shamanism—speaking in tongues—dredging the psychosphere—acting as mediums in something close to automatic writing—
　　　to regroup: the traditional shaman relates to the pomo writer in being a medium (the pomo writer preferring the medium to the well done)—medium between the dream world and the waking world, the psychic world and the so-called real world, tradition and contemporaneity, the dead and the living—a conduit between otherwise mutually exclusive forces—the shaman doesn't manufacture consciousness as smithy like modernist Joyce—s/he's more modestly a mediator—in a consumer culture shamans are bound to produce

new, unpackageable culture integrations that go against the grain of the efficiency oriented profit system by reintroducing disruptive forces that the system needs to exclude—artist as shaman therefore, often despite hiserself, oppositional in stance.

That's where Degenerative Prose comes in—Degen prose as a description of a new intergeneric synthesis of narrative writing encourages the breakdown of traditional genres and even mediums, like video and sonic—a mode particularly compatible with the ongoing shamanic role of ongoing recombination of the fragments of our culture—a culture already tessellated, if you know what i mean—that is, consisting of pieces that now fit together like mosaic tiles held in place mostly by force of economic necessity—the pomo shaman shattering those pieces and recombining them in mosaics more intrinsically coherent—Degen breaks down the arbitrary configurations of conglomerate culture, which as new multinational ambiance imposes its conditions on the literary/political situation—conglomerate culture through various means, writing its own script—or having it written—for the ongoing cultural narrative—the task of Degen being to unwrite that script—Degen's language being rhetorical/narrative rather than philosophical/logical—remembering that rhetoric is the language of debate and change while logic that of conclusion and pronouncement.

One manifestation of the intergensynth is the minimovement called Avant Pop—AvPo manipulates conglom formulations in a way akin to the Situationist ploy of detournement—using mass market forms—noir, horror, porn, etc.—to undercut mass market, altering them in subversive ways, loading them with oppositional messages and releasing them into the culture like computer viruses.

Implicit in Degen in late Pomo—a.k.a., Nomo (Nomo Pomo)—is Interventive Fiction. Interventive Ficton relates to Brechtian ideas about theater—as Surfiction usurped the ideology of realism, displacing its sense of imitating experience with surfictionist idea of adding to experience, so Interventive Fiction supplants Surfiction with its tactic of intervening in experience—where Surfiction was relatively passive and contemplative in its stance toward experience, and in this sense still esthetically oriented, Intervent is aggressive, interactive, influencing the course of event, changing attitudes, leading to action or even itself overflowing into overt gesture, performance, theater, or practical organization, including its own production and distribution—the continuum of effects in Intervent running from meditation to demonstration in all senses of the word.

8

Remember: the struggle of literature is to move constantly beyond literature, beyond the definitions of particular linguistic realities, beyond language itself, to change the world we live in.

from Phosphor in Dreamland

RIKKI DUCORNET

For two days Fango Fantasma had been silent. Indeed, Fogginius' conversation was so congested, infrangible, and dense that, had he wanted to, Fantasma would have been hard pressed to stick a word in, even edgewise. However, Fantasma shared Phosphor's baleful propensity and was not eager to talk. He had fallen to staring at his own reflection in a pocket mirror—not from vanity as might be supposed, but to reassure himself that he was still there. The farther away he went from familiar things, the more fragmented and permeable he felt himself to be—and the more haunted. The woods, the sea, the sky, the relic path under his mule's vanishing feet appeared to percolate to transparency.

Fantasma's unstable state of mind had been precipitated by a worsening pecuniary crisis. For several years he had hounded the papal authorities for permission to import Africans to work his mines and plantations. When at last his wish had been granted, he spent the lion's part of his languishing fortune to build and equip a ship, which, upon its return from Africa, its cargo chained and bolted to the hold, had been made to vanish—perhaps by those evil spirits that had plagued his line for three generations. It seemed to Fantasma, as the very clouds appeared to plot against him overhead, that he and his family had always been the playthings of witches.

Fogginius had once told Señor Fantasma that at the world's edge lived a people born riddled with holes. This peculiar race amused themselves by plugging their perforations with sod and planting them with roses.

"More often than not the wedding night ends in disaster," Fogginius told Fantasma, "for in their frenzied state the lovers—decked head to foot in thorny briars—tear one another to shreds."

"Such is the way of love—" Phosphor, eavesdropping, was cut to the quick by the story. He made up a little list of rhymes to keep for later: thorn/sworn, latch/patch, fur/burr, thistle/whistle.*

---

*The descent into the female vortex is vertiginous, writes Ombos, and culminates in the revelation of that vile machine, that reeking chest;

This night Fantasma felt like a sieve man; he felt that his substance was seeping out through the pores of his skin. To make matters worse, their finger of rock above the whirlpool—if certified by an auspicious dropping—was possibly haunted. Certain signs—caricatural boles and an abandoned wasp's nest—implied that they had tied their hammocks between what had once been sacred trees.

As their fire died, Fantasma stretched and, pulling on his fingers one by one until they popped, thought about Phosphor's ocularscope. He imagined himself enthroned upon a velvet chair, turning a crank that would yield up the island image after image.

Too agitated to sleep, Fantasma told himself the story of the nun who had neglected to cross herself before eating a banana. That failing, he attempted to bring to mind the tender moments of his infancy, but could only recall those family stories that, since cognizance, profoundly distressed him. Stories of those unstable ghosts taking root, tall as trees, in the dining room, causing the roast beef to explode; hovering near the birthing chair whenever a Fantasma was born, to snap up the umbilical cord the instant it was cut.

And then Fantasma thought he heard his own cord, and the cords of his forefathers, being pulled along the ground. He moaned and clutched his balls in terror; above the roar of the whirlpool, he heard one thousand phantoms stepping among the stones and breathed an air thick with the smoke of one thousand cigars.

Fantasma shivered. A clammy air rose up from under him; it mouthed his bones and caused his teeth to hammer. When the moon's thin wafer pulled itself up over the horizon, he peered timidly out from under his blanket, thinking to catch a glimpse of the ghosts that—he could hear them distinctly—were spooking the campsite. What he saw caused him to scream with such conviction the others were wrenched from sleep to see that the world beneath was no longer solid but palpitating with hundreds of thousands of frogs. The indigenous population had called the place above the whirlpool *Tlöck*. Indeed, as the frogs advanced snapping gnats, the

---

Celia's own Pandora's Box: her chamber pot—which, as Groddeck has pointed out, when stained with menstrual blood, is for the little boy an emblem of castration—or rather, the proof that the female is a castrated male. Celia's chamber pot, like the Brobdingnagian wench's vulva, is a metaphor for the Medusa herself: This cave...this gulph insatiable... the sight that turns a man to stone. It is no accident that the Nanunculus' intimate view of a frolicsome girl's outsized cabinet—a mirror of his own incapacities—is followed by the sight of a decapitation which in a fit of lyricism Gulliver likens to the jet d'eau of Versailles: an extravagant ejaculation, to say the very least.

11

party heard distinctly the percussive sound of their feasting: *Tlöck, tlöck, tlöck.*

Transfixed with terror, Fantasma sailed that amphibious sea howling as Yahoo Clay, more naked than any ape, waded among the little red and gold and green bodies, battering them with a club. Phosphor sat transfixed, Pulco wept, and Fogginius beat the air and cried:

"The magic is severe! My net's dissolved!" And then: "A dream! A dream and an oracle! We must count them!" The saint dropped to the ground and, fumbling among the frogs, raved: "Fallen from the sky! Clay! Desist! You are smattering the brains of rational angels!"

They finished the night prostrate but wakeful. It seemed to them that the entire cosmos reeked of mildew, stagnant pools, the shit of fish, the saliva of snakes, and the sulfurous flatulence of saints. Sometime before dawn, the frogs vanished into thin air—supporting Fogginius' thesis.

*

Ved, surely you recall a red tower, freakish and austere; built of a bloody marble imported from Spain, it shadows a squalid corner of the Old Quarter. Here Rais Secundo, his piles perpetually festering, gnawed his knuckles and plotted a world as seamless and silent as a saucer. His chamber, too, was of marble and perfectly round. (Secundo feared corners, shadows, and recesses of any kind.) This chamber brings to mind a tomb, and according to the tourist guide should be seen at midnight. In that ghostly hour, the place reeks of ill fortune. And although the Church can no longer claim the authority it had in Secundo's time, still the adjacent cathedral contains more gold than the wealth of all the island brought together, its gutters more copper and its treasure-house more silver, pearls, and brocade. (Yet the priest continues to panhandle after hard cash, badgering his flock—fisherfolk, mostly, weavers and such who worship in rags.)

What I'm getting at is this: the very week Fantasma and his party set off to seize the island by necromancy, Rais Secundo called a meeting of the Doctors of the Church and his Inquisitional Officers to discuss urgent matters. This list was long. He was hot after smoke and itching for pyres; he craved the stench of sinners roasting.*

---

*According to Ombos, once the Church had created a Hell of roaring flames, it was inevitable it would then set about roasting sinners on earth—an imagined Hell the inspiration and the justification.

Now, it was assumed by the Powers that if the Christ had both masticated and swallowed, *he did not digest.* Once food hit Christ's stomach it vaporized like water on hot coals. But several days before the departure, as he sat beside Yahoo Clay jabbering deep into the night, Fogginius perfected the argument that Christ produced an excrement in every way like that of every man. Later, in the streets and marketplace, he labored his conviction to all who would listen and was heard by Secundo's infallible spies.

Fogginius' argument went like this: if God gave his son a physical body the better to punish him, surely that body which—it was documented—bled and perspired—digested, too. Fogginius had himself seen the Lord's foreskin in Barcelona under glass. He reasoned: if the Lord had a virile member, he surely urinated; if he urinated, surely he shat. And did that not prove excrement was a good, a natural thing? So necessary in gardens and love potions alike?

This abominable argument was overheard by three shuddering and credible witnesses. Fogginius' abandoned hovel, its floor a rampart of clumped and rotted things, was visited by Rais Secundo himself. He came back with an awful look in his eyes and described the hole as hot with heresy and as pagan as an African bazaar overrun with devils black and brown.

He had the place spattered with holy salt and then he set it on fire.

According to the records, so many devils perished in that fire they left a pool of rancid butter thirty feet across and three thumbs deep. This butter was collected, filtered, poured into blue bottles, and kept as proof of sorcery. Awaiting the wizard's capture, Secundo arranged the bottles on his windowsill where, against the day, they cast blue reflections. Toying with his deadly instruments impatiently, Secundo bitterly complained: "All the pins and thumbscrews in God's universe can't nail a witch who has flown the coop!" These infamous words were taken up by children:

> *Thumbscrew, thumbscrew*
> *Ducking stool.*
> *Bleed sir, bleed sir,*
> *Buckets full.*

and

> *Pin and pillory*
> *Gibbet and noose,*

Catch the witches
As they roost.
If they wake and fly away,
Roast them on another day.

The blue bottles were said to have a weird influence on those who saw them. A novitiate of the Order of Rosy Water was quietly conversing with the Inquisitor in his tower when he was suddenly seized in the fist of a fit and sent a piping pot of tea into Secundo's lap.

Eupoetics* (A Parallel Manifesto)

EURUDICE

1. I will never imitate nature and beauty, because I'd never rob me of my own *awe*—what else do I live for? Leave the monkeying tricks to the money-raking itinerant crowd pleasers; true magic has nothing to do with mimesis. I want to do the opposite of what nature can do. (I don't interfere with nature, and I hope nature doesn't with my text.)

2. I mostly interfere with culture, the old logos-animus, the more masculine and less sublime axis. My aim is to help pass the culture through the sieve, collect the actual glossolalic seeds and reshape them not into the soft Galatea I'd like (I'm forever fighting my Pygmalion complex) but Medusa, whose splendid head it pleases me to be turning out to confront the world as its mirror-*du-jour*. I believe seeing is the opposite of believing.

3. I like to see language as a healing tool and metaphor as cathartic as any violence. The achievement of the ancient tragedies was to purge by causing pity-and-fear (i.e., *culture*-inspired *awe*); even though a thousand years of soap operas have fatally mutated the genre, it is that brutal power of the word I aspire to. If I didn't abhor new ageisms, I'd say for me writing is shamanistic—meant to exorcise demons and overpower *common sense*. As it is, I'll just say that literature keeps me from feeling unceasingly ridiculous.

4. I have no interest in realism, because I'm so interested in reality. Reality is unspeakable, I think, which is why I write, to stretch the language to express the fringes of what's real (it's the "last three clauses of the *Unnamable*" syndrome). Reality is the echo of a timebound smell that can't be deciphered. Reality is an ancient mammoth Klein bottle filled to the brim with *sound and fury* from which there is only cerebral escape. I don't really know memory. I'd like to know "the one word that rips apart the world."

5. Writing helps me face my mortality which I live to overcome. Writing saves me from my female onus and absolves me from my body's limitations. Finally, fiction is my way of usurping the making of history from the bullies-that-be.

---

* "creating well" in Greek

6. All my writing is an act of rebellion. I couldn't stay sane and articulate, or intelligibly clad and mannered, if I didn't release words. In another era I might have been a woman possessed by satans, sooner or later burned on some sort of stake. (But I'm alive, now, at the ball, waiting for Godot, in a society still itching to cover up my shame.)

7. Because language in the mouth of a woman can be deadly, preliterate, alchemical (woman is literacy's untouchable, an ineffable catalyst in reaction to which language was created and which continues to prove its inadequacy), it can both undermine the stability of any sacred cow and turn into a potentially "natural" language that bridges any distance.

8. I can only live as a foreigner. It is an honest *modus* that highlights my difference, freeing for I am never expected to know and follow the mores of the locals. It allows for a relative degree of ignorance and naiveté that punctures life's hot air balloon. I obsess and write about America as I see it from an inside-the-seams outsider's point of view, because its ideology has the ominous power to permeate and homogenize the rest of the world. I'd like my writing to span the lonely treacherous soul of America. English is not my first language; this allows me to hear it objectively, free sign from referent, use and abuse the vernacular without the learned or sentimental hesitations and respect for vast traditions that restricted me in my own tongue; I purposefully write in American because it is the Latin of the postmodern world. Every writer is an outsider; and all human activity is a striving after the wind, so those less weighty catch up the best. I write best as an exile.

P.S.—There is no greater art than the art of daily life. The talent for living well is the most substantial; so I try to fashion my *life* as I would create a text, driven by sheer desire and imagination, with no regard to rules, limits or fears, feasting on this bottomless world.

(Meanwhile, let us not forget the lofty cosmos hovering upstairs)

1. Realism—our gigantic linguistic compromise—made our madness comprehensible (and comprehensive) and propagated an illusion of order by defining its codes and norms, until Modernism eloquently mourned our loss of romance and conquest, and the abrupt end of "accurate" perception, and soon after, Postmodernism celebrated our chaos, rejoicing in its newly begotten perverted cynicism (John Barth, for instance, has made a career of reveling in the death of every literary genre); the text was written in order not to mean but to be. Most postmodernists fetishized the structure and

epistemology, instead of the epiphany. No longer. Today we're primarily interested in the irreducible clean nonverbal revelation, the intuition, not the analysis. We now perceive the classical and the innovative as synonyms. We've played "connect the dots" so often since Rimbaud, that we're impatient; especially as *our* continuous present is taking us straight into the cascading millennium (maybe an unimaginable renaissance). Sartre was happy to spend life looking out the back window of a moving car, seeing everything present as having happened already. We'd rather *act up* our writing; so we hide less, want more, face proudly the failing world of which we're symptoms, walk our talk and talk as prophets. The new writer is an apocalypsist.

2. But can we listen? Less and less, as the info-assaults escalate and what used to be communication is war. Myth means to us "untrue." The only lies we can still stomach are our own. (Only what we can consume can we trust; the edible is the new Muse.)

3. Dante distinguished all words between *pexa et hirsuta*, the hairy and the combed (the punks and the preppies). Breton, simplifying matters, said that a real writer is one who takes a gun, goes down in the street and randomly fires at the crowd until the gun is empty.

4. If you juxtapose W. C. Williams' dictum "No ideas but in things" to Rene Girard's assertion "Language stops where reality starts," and Henry James' "The only thing we can demand of a novelist *per se* is that he should be interesting" to Gertrude Stein's "You can write masterpieces only when you are not you as your little dog knows you," you get Baudelaire's "A writer must be both a somnambulist and a hypnotist"; a simple equation.

5. Joyce and Proust show us that all trivial men are transcendental and thus eternal (i.e., "instantaneous"), so regardless of our ever achieving freedom from identity and unleashing the forbidden text beneath the surface, our battlefield must always remain the world's great banal surface. A surface is like Conrad's rotting river: we penetrate it to find it is impenetrable. Something is always fleeting: that is the essence of all writing. (To implicate Hegel, a. Thesis: all is in order, and b. Antithesis: nothing is in order, leads to: c. Synthesis: there is order which lacks a center, and that missing link—the little wailing gorilla—drives our need to tell every story. That is, to pose the question: "Why am I not a chimpanzee?")

6. For as Nietzsche and Derrida make clear, we have to posit a center to say anything; so as the surrounding structure develops we find there is no center, yet keep chasing it (good old rainbow); for "God" is a game player forever dividing the universe, and once we catch on, realize that the division is false and start uniting the parts as

"God" separates them, we transcend; for the self is a stray animal being chased (caught between loss and recovery, hunger and disgust). All in all, I think literature not only is not conveniently representative of any society or even of a rebellion against that society, but that if in its unpredictability it is representative of anything, it is representative of the nonrepresentative; it is resistance.

7. Or, as Colette said of love, a primordial battle. All love is quotation; on the other hand, love teaches us more about creating fiction than anything else in life, because it can always be urgent, new & arousing. That's why love-lust is the lens I use to understand the world.

8. Which leads me to womanhood: In this late-twentieth, the use of love as a means of socially normalizing women has declined, and women are producing their own virtuoso seduction texts that are direct coital acts. Phallic penetration of the woman's vaginal ear is no longer the sweeping function of language. Unfortunately, no disenfranchised voice can avoid being appropriated by the *status quo* once it is defined as art. As soon as it acquires any prestige and power, it loses all potency (look at Duchamp or Basquiat). To be potent, art must be able to decay before it can be consumed and canonized; it *must* be apocryphal. The author must denounce it as failure as soon as it is made public. Once you enter the fancy gates, you're the sultan's eunuch before-you-know-it. The sultan doesn't make love, or money, or *jihad*; he collects taxes and spends them to make puppets of himself; only those who stay out of the cozy palace can see the strings holding everyone up and recognize his intimate chuckle: this short cautionary metaphor was my earliest childhood fiction, a product of both phobia and imagination, with the former using the latter to justify itself.

P.S.—Every notion of progress is refuted by the *Iliad*, a text that was a perfect act of provocation and defiance toward the waves of lesser articulation in the centuries to come. We're still trying to match its sharp and lucid radiance that has been shaping our world.

(Nor the barbarous yawn gaping beyond)

It strikes me that I'm Avant-Pop simply because my writing is the equivalent of:

1. staying pregnant forever, ever since I unexpectedly found myself,
2. running from the earth-churning tanks deafeningly firing at everyone around me in the familiar crowded streets before the sealed-off University and slipping on spilled blood,

3. and later that night pulling up my nightgown under the heavy sweaty covers as a twelve year old and whispering to the cavernous dark, "Fuck me! Fuck me! Please..," frantically,

4. then taking to the air lifted by my billowing hunger high over the old city battlements,

5. fleeing the immense windblown waiting room of the dead, escaping from the circle of my existence as if from a crime, and, burden-free, sinking my claws back into the earth,

6. feeling for the first time a man's eyelashes batting against my labia, as if I were flayed,

7. and afterwards lying smeared silver with sperm inside a foreign boy's daydream,

8. while tracking the awesome white speck of an insect making its way busily over a beauty mark and through the fine hairs on my left arm tickling me lightly as I was scribing this.

P.S.—"Even a dunce leaps out of bed, inspired."
    Sherwood Anderson

(to be continued)

SIM2\RE.LA.VIR:
She Watches, Channel Φ

JAN EMILY RAMJERDI

my cunt lips hang down so low they could be balls. "you're hanging out" "i like . . . so . . . ummm . . . i like to hang out— here: smell" i touch myself, run my fingers through LA.BUM and hold my fingers to my nose, then i put them in my mouth.

ick   you're such a lesbian
and you?
what
what what
what?

what?   you're not?

turn around

         Suture

    Suture What: (it's the old ΦI.BITe:

    To What: I.chBI.ndigitIT.el(ΦII.BIT.IT)::
                    fff:fff:ff&f
        fist fuck&font)

it takes a long time

i use the WD-40 and wedge-one wand from RE.LA.VIR's

oβoλUTILItyBOx:

_____

❑ Φ.LOVe.RE.LA.VIR

_____   **(i like branches)**

❏ Φ.LIVe.RE.LA.VIR

_____   **(i like branches,**
_____
_____ **to   (o)**
        To What: **t oo)**

I like branches.
I like branches in their detail.
I like branches curved in exquisite lines bent by the winds constantly blowing through them.
I like branches to be bent in a way relating.
I like branches to be women.
I like branches to follow what I think.
I like branches two at a time.
I like never parting branches.

O.K. We'll hold our position here among the birds.
They like branches.

This is how they are in Spring.
It is no longer Spring now.

My fondest thoughts are of you Cherry.
Things change, Little Red Leaf.

3. Now is now . . .

&i don't like branches anymore&i don't like to branch to anymore&anyway what the fuck do branches branch to when they branch to any kind of fucking air?

Suture

Suture What: i went to the Palac
e i wore   d ark cri mson rubb
er appliance to assfuck glos glos glos
sed silk i want to 8
over eight

To What: thin knots under robes of dark red
8 knots of drk rd slk glos glos 8 & 8
glos gls & sht 8 8 gls & sht eight knts slk & sht slk & sht
gls gls sht gls 8 & 8 sht 8 sht 8 & 8sht8sht8sht8&8sht
sht8&8sh8sh t

option≠bold

SELECT SPEED OPTION = S(t) = S(t-1)**(1/ß)
          where:
                    S(t)= Speed in time t
                     S(t-1) = Speed in time t-1
                     ß>0= Fixed unknown PARAMeter

shhhhhh   pfffsssssst   shhh   just o to sleep just
o pfffffst pfffst   to sleep shhhhhh they found pieces of
ffffffffft fffffffft bo dy shhhht   shhht   shhhh shhhh
          just   o to   sssssbo   dy   they   found
          pieces of shhhhht shhhht shhhhhhh's body just
o to just o to just o to sleee   they found pieces of
pieces of shhhht sht shhht's bo   dy
they found pieces of shhhh shh shhhh's   bod
          y
just o to just o to just o to sleep just o to just o to just o to
sleep just o to

RE.VOLVE.HER>>RE.VULVE.HER>>RE.VALVE.HER
>>RE.VIRVE.HER>>FUCK>>FUCK>>HER>>HERE
IS   WHERE   I   FUCK   HER>>RE.VIRV>>HER>>
FUCK>>IN>>RE.VOLVE.HER>>NOW>>IT'S>>YOUR>>
TURN>>NOW>>RE.VIRV>>RE.VIRV>>RRR>>
RRRRR>>RE>>RE>>RE>>VERT>>

when i come i tear the corners of her mouth

because i make her
let me

I rape her because

i make her
let me

dear reaDER.WRI.ter(WRI.DER) of the

To What:	queerpurple Open:	SAGE:
	☐ somedayyou	
	☐ somedayyou	will
	☐ somedayyou	
	☐ somedayyou	will

(get the K-Y)

Welcome to Some Day You Will Rape Like I Rape™

You have just entered TEMPL.micro::somedayyouwill
@TEMPL.MAC.RO::SO.DO.ME™RiV.etSEX.tinc.

If you need instructions, just touch the screen!

☞index or fist

enter (password): (✿✳▲✳✳✳■❖○✳✳❱▲✳▲✳✳○▲■■✎)

[NARR.TRANS.DOC: (she was a whore before)]

Welcome to RE.dLA.VIRtualhypernovel—RE.LA.VIR!

The following instructions on how to read
RE.dLA.VIRtualhypernovel, RE.LA.VIR, will help you
fully experience your first VIRtualhypernovel. If you have

questions that are not answered here, consult user docu-
mentation (USE.DOC) on the DOC disks:
VIRtualDICtionary (VIR.DIC.DOC), GLOSS.DOC,
SouRCeDOC, NARR.EXPLIC&TRANS.DOCs.

Technical consultants (B.E.T.T.A.SSiSts: βicon) are available to assist you 24-hours 7 days a week (1-900-COP-
AINS $5.03 first min. $3.91 each min after).

If you are equipped with a modem, (just touch the screen)
simply highlight the passage you need HELP? w/ and you
will be automatically connected with one of our
B.E.T.T.A.SSSs (βicon (see: Show TI.ME, Show $)).

RE.LA.VIR Features: (-)

– TEMPL.eAcceSSfiles:ϖ//TEMPL.ASSs\\ϖ

ϖ//TEMPL.ASSs\\ϖ are designed to assist the
WRI.terreaDER:℘ WRI.DER℘ in navigating through
♥ |∅RE.LA.VIR∅| ♥. They provide easy access to, from,
and in, between, individual ΩTEMPLsΩ and multiple
NarraTiveTemplE.N.E.TWoRkS™.

βicon   enter her through the backdoor

ΦI.VAN☞you know the one   the☞Terrible: the beauty
as was fucked   9. CUNT, too,

queenie, you're a virtual NO.NO.vel cunt too, RE.LA.VIR,
a VIR.tualVIR. alSmoothSpace(VIR.VIR.SS) too to spread
my body organs in to every piece of your mouth

   i tear the corners of her mouth when i come
                        I am filling in to the color
RE.d, LA. VIR. tu. al HYP. er. NO.NO!vel a LA.REd, in
fragmenta, RE.LA.VIR   and glue too and then too large
enough memory of you to you ME.MORE.X CD-WOM-an:

We recommend at least 4MB RAm (preferably 8MG) jerdi, a sound card, and speakers. of you to
youof you to
I occupy you Φ I fill you in and equation you, equation by equation, you equation you, and cunt too, **queenie YOU'RE A FUCKIN' CUNT TO,** Φ equation and cunt too, cunt to cunt yours and mine **I'm a fuckin' cunt too,** Φ cunt and equation paste too cunt to cunt cunt to cunt to ass too gel and glue too I gel and glue and gel and glue to **GLUE AND PASTE TO YOU. I got a cunt gun to.** cuntgun to. I got a cuntgun to. I got a cuntgun to I got a cuntgun too and I'm gonna paste you paste you and I'm gonna cunt and paste and cunt and paste you and I you and Icunt Icunt and paste and paste and paste you and **I SHUT YOU UP BITCH you in your fucking pennsylvamnia YOU IN YOUR FUCKING TEMPL:MAC. RO::PENNSYLVAMNIA** you and your up on micro queenie you and your up on micro in and in yours **IN YOURS in your own little black hole, your're in IN IN I AM IN TO AND UP** your own little black hole queenie, I'm gonna paste you in with you queenie for a day, then I'm gonna roll you over and I'm gonna roll you over and I'm gonna roll you over and king you I'm gonna king you queenie ass backwards for a day bend over get on your knees and micro, **I'M GONNA** widen you **I'M GONNA MAC.RO YOU** your large enough too and insert a whole ferry boat **DRY TOO,** bow and aft, bow and aft lift your aft and **RE.**ad too doodle doo doodle doo doo doodle **LA LA** here's how it is: **VIR.** doodle doo and graffiti too here's my graffitti to spray it up your ass, scratch scratch and sniff up your bowel walls

Both Feeds in the Middle Kingdom (*from* Once Upon a Time in China: "Jade Pork")

STEVE KATZ

The Imperial Museum in Taipei exhibits Jade Pork. This is one of the greatest museums of the world. Whatever I think of the old Mandarin dictatorship in Taiwan, I still thank Chiang Kai-Shek and cohorts for having carried these cultural riches away with them when they fled the communists. This feeling is reinforced once I see on the mainland how much was mutilated, neglected, or destroyed, especially during the cultural revolution. Anything that was worth moving, and could be moved to Taiwan, the Nationalists took with them. So this Imperial Museum brims with the whole treasure of Chinese Civilization. You can spend forever looking at the paintings, or the bronzes, or the jade.

From the endless jade collection the most prized single piece, among all the chalices and bowls exquisitely carved, the cooly glowing bracelets and hair-pieces figured with elaborate detail, is one simple hunk of jade carved to resemble a slab of pork. I'm not kidding. A slab of pork! This isn't just another of the many pieces, but the most treasured one. Jade pork. It sits in its own glass cube, in its own case, on its own pedestal, lit softly with a spot from the ceiling. It is thick as a slab of pork prepared simply for a banquet, a layer of snowy white fat covering a layer of grey-pink pork meat. Those are the shades I felt I saw, that I remember of it, though its real colors are two tones of translucent jade green, paler above, greyish below. The textures are perfect, creamy on the top layer, densely fibrous below. It lies as if it has just been placed there for the banquet, never really carved in jade, but never prepared either from the flesh of a beast. It arrives every moment fresh at the banquet of the mind, and has done so forever, an inedible eight inch square of firm edible pork.

It's not as unimpressive as it sounds, and that's the mystery of it. It has presence and holds your attention with an odd nobility that captures the mind in echoes of gustatory sensuality, a mineral lusciousness, unattainable gratification. You feel the weight of it on your brain stem. It doesn't let your attention skip. With your eyes you taste the difference between the flesh and the fat, feel the transition in your bite from one texture to the other. Here I am, I recollect myself, staring at a piece of pork, and it's just a rock, I say, so why am I held by it, as if it were some different rock, like the Michelangelo David?

In the case next to it there's an almost equally prized jade piece sculpted as a head of bok choy, very light and cabbagey, with perfect jade crickets sitting on it, everything about two-thirds life size. Its detail is intricate and exact, carved from one slab of jade, crickets included, a piece of astounding virtuousity; but the simple hunk of pork is more potent, holds my attention, remains in my imagination. Is this thing some early Chinese pop art? Not that. There's no campiness here, no social commentary here, nothing satirical. This isn't one of Wayne Thiebaud's juicy paintings of a wedge of cake, that makes you think about <u>excess</u>. It's not a soft Claes Oldenburg burger or one of his wilting electric toothbrushes, making fun of the impotence of power. It's not an Andy Warhol pop icon reproduced in the context of "high art", that makes you confront the iconography of the culture. This is a serious piece of pork. Just pork, no talk. And it's not a *nature morte*, like the sumptuous Dutch and Flemish paintings of the 17th Century, still-lifes full of game fowl and venison, fruits, cheeses, vegetables, sumptuous fabrics, ornate objects. It's not about the luscious light reflected off wealth, testifying to the empowerment in the material world of a rising middle class. This is perpetual pork, a feeling of ready-to-eat, a piece of jade sculpture. A portion of cold stone. Get your legs under the table, pilgrim, and celebrate forever the pleasures of the table. And this is jade, prized for its quality of remaining cold to the touch, even on the hottest days, that paradox being one of its healing properties.

*   *   *   *   *

One evening while strolling in Taipei with my son and his future wife, Jade Wisdom, we pass a ceremony taking place under a canopy on a busy shopping street, a solemn ritual carved into crowds and traffic. On a raised platform under the canopies a priest sits, occasionally chanting. Two of his monks sit beside him, ringing bells. A number of nuns, dressed in saffron and grey ceremonial robes, sit on the pavement in front of him, singing, playing finger bells, and simple bowed instruments, like drones. The music, leeching into the traffic noise, is strange, hypnotic, beautiful; perfect for the lassitude of a humid Taipei evening. Jade Wisdom explains that this is a Daoist funeral, though it is hard these days to tell the difference between Daoist and Buddhist ceremony. The sons of the deceased, their heads hidden under brown paper bags, stand facing the priests with incense burners in their hands. The music and the smell of sandalwood separate the ceremony from the commerce. Some shops adjacent are shuttered and Jade Wisdom speculates they belong to the family of the deceased; but the rest of the street is packed with business as usual, traffic indifferent to the ceremony.

Spread on an enormous table under one of the canopies is a great exhibition of food. This is an exquisite feast, everyone's dream of the best Chinese banquet — a whole turkey in a hazel glaze, looking like a precious stone, a split pig's head sauced and sumptuous, lobster and shrimp layed out in elaborate mandalas, platters of shining snails and cracked sea urchins, bubbling chafing dishes of various mysteries, an array of doufou in its endless forms, bowls of savory vegetables, and snowy heaps of rice. It looks to me like the family is going to have a great mourning feast of remembrance, a terrific idea, I think; but this is a different idea. Jade Wisdom says they don't eat the food. This is ceremonial. It sits outside and slowly spoils, and passes into the other world with the spirit of the dead man, for him to share at table with his ancestors on the other side. The living are left to watch this voluptuous but ephemeral banquet pass on with the soul of their relative, reassured by what will always remain for the living, and even for the dead, the pleasures of the rituals of jade pork.

EIGHT
ADULT
MALES

A NEUROPSYCHOLOGICAL
DRAMA

Norman Conquest
&
Derek Pell

Dramatis Personae

Dave, *an adult male*   Larry, *an adult male*

Zeke, *an adult male*   Shorty, *an adult male*

Riva, *an adult male*   Arnie, *an adult male*

Herby, *an adult male*   Benny, *an adult male*

ACT ONE

A laboratory somewhere in Southern California. Curtain rises on eight adult males prior to any surgical intervention.

DAVE
(dominant, self-
assured, feared)

ZEKE
(aggressive,
attacker)

RIVA
(aggressive,
active)

HERBY
(placid,
unassertive)

LARRY
(submissive,
cowering, frequently
attacked)

SHORTY
(submissive to
others, aggressive
towards Larry)

ARNIE
(noisy,
eager)

BENNY
(alert, active
food getter)

ACT TWO

The laboratory, a few days later. Same as Act One, except that a bilateral amygdalectomy has been performed on Dave.

ZEKE
(dominant)

RIVA
(daring, competes)

HERBY
(indifferent)

BENNY
(indifferent)

ARNIE
(indifferent)

SHORTY
(active)

LARRY
(dominates &
attacks Dave)

DAVE
(completely
submissive)

ACT THREE

The laboratory, a few days later. Same as Act Two, except that both Dave and Zeke have received bilateral amygdalectomies.

RIVA
(dominant, not
threatened by others)

HERBY
(passive)

BENNY
(passive)

ARNIE
(passive)

LARRY
(alert)

SHORTY
(active)

ZEKE
(avoids
interaction)

DAVE
(submissive)

ACT FOUR

The laboratory, a few days later. Sames as the first three acts, except that Dave, Zeke, Riva, Herby, Larry, Shorty, Arnie, and Benny have all received bilateral amygdalectomies.

RIVA
(inactive)

HERBY
(inactive)

BENNY
(inactive)

ARNIE
(inactive)

LARRY
(inactive)

SHORTY
(inactive)

ZEKE
(inactive)

DAVE
(inactive)

The SprayGun Mondo Vanilli interview

Ken Dorfberg

MV SELLS OUT! EXCRETING MEDIA...
OR JUST THE SAME OLD SHIT?

Mondo Vanilli is a very peculiar rock band, if that's in fact what they are. Pretending to be a pure media prank, they started their career with the False Starts Tour—a series of canceled performances. In interviews in various cyberpunk zines, the ubiquitous R. U. Sirius spoke of MV as pure concept and purveyed his philosophy that any concept is ruined when you attempt to realize it.

But with the release of IOU Babe on Naught/Innerscop Records, we have a respectable—actually rather extraordinary—CD. This 65 minutes of actual (as opposed to virtual?) music, dialog and... *advertisements* is composed and performed (or so they claim) by band members: the aforementioned R. U. Sirius, Scrappi DüChamp, and Simone 3Arm.

The album is a grab-bag of hard techno and technopop styles unified by a sort of avant garde cinematic approach to the concept album. The fragments of dialog that ride on top of some musical segments sound like a cinematic voice track. Advertisements connect some of the songs. Overall, one gets the sense of listening to what might be a noir movie musical—a fragmented story about; macho posturing (Sirius), sarcastic feminine power (3Arm), the nagging conscience of the post-modern artist/thief (Sirius and DüChamp), and constipation and excrement as metaphors for politics and art (3Arm and DüChamp)—all done up as Theater of the Ridiculous. Songs range from hip-hype dance hit material like Thanx! *and* Love is the Product *to the ambient Eno-esque* Clones Don't Have to be so Cold *to the Psycho-Industrial terror of* Gimme Helter.

So I'm waiting for MV, whatever they are, at the Cafe Fnord, South of Market in San Francisco. Sirius arrives first for the interview, only fifteen minutes late, wearing black jeans and a black turtleneck. He seems distracted and orders a cup of cappuccino. After a few minutes of small talk, he fixes me in his sights and gives me the ground rules. He'd rather not talk about his history with MONDO 2000 "and all that." And—here's the bomb—the band doesn't really want to talk about the album. They'll talk about the upcoming Fucking Robot Tour, they'll talk about their ideas and theories, themselves… whatever. But not the album. "Once something is done, what you think it means is more important than what we think it means. And the usual rock-and-roll stuff about musicianship and who did what in the studio and all… forget it." He gets that out just as 3 Arm and DüChamp arrive.

3 Arm's shocking-pink hair is shaved toward the top of her head where she has a tattoo of a white picket fence. She's wearing a kind of silver spacesuit with inappropriate (at least for a street café) holes. Her smile is as wide and bright as the warm California sun, as she asks me… how I like the album. "We're not going to talk about the album," I mutter into my coffee cup. "Oh yeah," she says. Scrappi, who is dressed up dandy-style in a powder blue cape, puffy-sleeved shirt and knife-creased pants seems ill at ease, and settles into the chair next to Sirius. Within minutes we're all armed with our favored caffeine. The MONDO Vanilli interrogation begins.

SprayGun: In the packaging for IOU Babe you offer Mondo Vanilli t-shirts with the slogan "Music is Obsolete." So isn't Mondo Vanilli obsolete?

R. U. Sirius: No. We're Sacred Monsters. We get to violate our own rules. As the Church of the SubGenius says, "I don't practice what I preach 'cause I'm not the kind of person that I'm preachin' *to.*" Think of it this way. MONDO Vanilli is absolute permission for the ultimate plastic rock-and-roll media institution, the first self-conscious post-punk faux subversive version of the Monkees. I think we're destined to hit the secret button on the masterplan fantasy of some bored executive.

SG: I understand that you actually performed only once before you got a record deal. Where was that?

Scrappi DüChamp: It was at Toontown in San Francisco. We were on a scissor lift that brought us 20 feet up in the air, with a torture bed that spun around, video projectors and jars of chocolate sauce. We hit people with fire extinguishers, scared them a bit… The peace authorities came to straighten things out.

RUS: We also played the R. U. Sirius-for-President '92 campaign party.

SG: How'd that go?

RUS: I don't think I won.

SD: I think you did. So now we are running a pig for the President of Outer Space.

Simone 3 Arm: You can have a cat, but you can't have a pig as a pet in the White House… I don't think.

SD: You can have a pig as a pet in the White House!
S3A: You can?
SD: It's been done.
SG: Why do you want a pet pig?
SD: Because they're like humans!
S3A: Yeah: they're selfish and they understand...
SG: So what's the Mondo Vanilli philosophy?
RUS: The goal is pure concept. When you try to actually achieve what you imagine, it ruins the whole thing.
SD: It's a little bit different from pure nihilism...
RUS: It's a very objective philosophy, actually...
SD: ...it's Mondo VaNihilism.

---

the only way you can achieve dada spontaneity in a high-tech surveillance society is by incorporating as a dadaist multinational.

RUS: We'd like to see franchised Mondo Vanilli bands in every city across this great land. They'll pay us dues and they'll BE Mondo Vanilli. There will be hundreds of Mondo Vanilli shows going on at once. Our preference is for Holiday Inn-style bands, but they can be anything they want.
SD: As long as they pay!
RUS: There's just so much freedom implicit in the name Mondo Vanilli. For instance, there's no reason that for our next record MV won't do a market study and hire professionals. They'll play according to market spec, and churn out hits in the prescribed style. In fact, it's implicit in MV that that *will* happen. Beyond that.

We'd also like to be the first media group to make signatured advertisement. In other words, we'd give ourselves credit in the closing few seconds. I predict that this will have a short but effective moment being *hot*. It's so *inevitable*.
SG: Is inevitability a valid reason for doing something?
RUS: I have no problem with that. What's worrying me is how and where we recontextualize the subversive impulse to keep it fresh and... relevant. The only way you can achieve dada spontaneity in a high-tech surveillance society is by incorporating as a dadaist multinational. The idea is this: people on the street can be totally random. And the more you climb up the social strata, the less random you can be and the more inhibited you become. But once you climb to the top of the ladder you can reverse that and become random again. I mean random from the perspective of Warner Brothers or Sony—just put out random shit that doesn't necessarily make

any sense. You can only get away with that on the top. Being random on the street, you're without access to the tools and the media. It's much more fun being random to twenty million people. I mean, Michael Jackson couldn't even kick in a car window on his fucking video and he was the king of fucking pop! So I'm trying to position Mondo Vanilli Corporation as a chaotic living system hooked to info-communication media extruding real and virtual stuff while deconstructing and exploiting marketing concepts under a brand name. It's one of many attempts to suck the whole sick bloody wonderful mess into a singular point, or a media black whole... ahh, as a prank.

SD: Mutate into mutiny! Do a prank, walk the plank. Kicking in a car window......sheesh. I liked the video where he raised the dead. Now THAT's kingly behavior!

SG: **Let's talk about the performance tour you guys are preparing for this winter. What's the "Fucking Robot Tour" going to be like?**

RUS: They'll be sort of like Erhardt Seminar Training sessions. Or boot camp. People are going to come, hopefully, all dressed in their leather outfits and sunglasses expecting another cool industrial music show just like every other one. And then, instead of darkness, they'll get the bright lights, and there will be these geeks in uniforms leading them to their folding chairs. For quite a while we'll just talk and show pictures. Like kind of a DE-program.

SD: We'll laser point to the vast array of Mondo Vanilli products and services... without getting too far into this... We have to keep it fairly secret or no one's going to want to come.

RUS: Then the rest of the show will revolve around the CyberPiss Goddess character. It's a comic book enactment of the legend of the CyberPiss Goddess of Annihilating Feces.

S3A: I want to have an Enema Bar.

RUS: We'll have a segment in our Fucking Robot performance tour where a small, elite group are invited into one of the bathrooms, which will become a performance venue. We'll show it live through a video hookup. It'll be like the other performance Simone did called "Smoking Fudge Pack."

S3A: We went into the audience and captured a cowboy, kidnapped him, tied him up, put him in the bathroom and gave him an enema. We showed it on ten video screens in the theater.

SG: **Simone, do you have a name for what you do?**

S3A. I'm an entertainment contortionist and an existential gender bender.

SG: Er, where do your performances ideas come from? Do you spend a lot of time thinking about them or do they just come to you in a flash?

S3A: It's always something that I'm obsessed with. I make it pretty simple and functional. You only need a few incongruous elements to make something very strange and effective.

R. U. was fascinated by the idea of the Enema paintings because it was so simple but challenging. I did my first Enema Performance onstage with my 50 year-old slave Jack Daniels, who happens to be a pre-op transsexual. She sat on a toilet seat that I put on stage—some kind of a porta-potty from a hospital—and I inserted an enema bag into her. I was wearing a medical uniform. I used grape juice and she released on a canvas that I put underneath the porta-potty. As she did that, I danced with my swords in a glittery outfit. It was very festive. I called the performance "Icky" and it really did make a mess. She didn't hold it as long as we expected.

After that I started working with Don Novello—Father Guido Sarducci—doing a Bad Catholic Girl skit with Lilly Braindrop. We would dress up like Catholic school girls, get into a girlfight on stage, tearing off each other's clothes. People enjoyed that.

Right around that time, I was learning Butoh, working with harupin-ha from Japan. And recently I started taking classes in trapeze. So now it's going to get a little more complex because I'm incorporating these abilities into my performance work. I have sort of childhood circus-like ideals with an extremely sadistic and twisted sense of humor. I use that to take the pretense out of today's performance art. I don't analyze too much. I just spew them out.

SG: So tell me about your cyberpiss character.

S3A: She's unfortunately a cartoon character and Earth is unfortunately a cartoon planet. She only gets one dimension. If she fucks a toaster, she becomes the toaster. She gets the toast off, but *so what*. She can't have a deep relationship, because the toaster can't become something else afterwards and she can. It's not a complex enough machine. There doesn't seem to be a complex enough hardware for her, with a brain that would stimulate her, because she's passionate and intelligent and she wants a component to turn her on, and to make her feel less lonely. Right now she's working for saving the constipated ape planet and all that, and that's OK. But y'know, she has to have some personal time... (laughs)

SG: What are a few of the other themes in this program? What can the audience expect to see that they'll clamor to buy tickets for?

S3A: Lots of visuals, multimedia... layered media. You'll feel that you are in a different world when you are in the theatre, like going to the Exploratorium. You'll be going into a world where there will be televisions everywhere with footage of toilets, toilet visuals that are very inventive and arty... alluring. A seduction at the end with the Fucking Robot—the Goddess meets her mate. It's like *The Last Tango in Paris*, only we lost Brando for a robot.

Simone Third Arm, as the Alien, is very concerned with Alienation and constipation. She wants to start a whole Bowel Movement. She wants people to release themselves.

SG: Gaaaaak... So do you relate human embarrassment about excrement to nationalism, racism and all those things, as the Post-Freudians do?

S3A: Wouldn't it be beautiful if we created one big toilet bowl and somebody from every country came and *shit together at the same time*. And just flushed... flushed all that tension... (singing) We are the world. We're on the toilet.

SG: I can't decide if this is going to be brilliant or embarrassing.

RUS: Both. Public embarrassment is the cutting edge of liberation. In a mass-mediated cyber-culture, the greatest risk is *embarrassment*. I mean, what're ya gonna do, virtual skydiving?....

SG: What about the romance with technology, the sex robot... and R. U., you've talked about getting plastic surgery on stage. Isn't technoculture driving us towards nightmarish conclusions?

RUS: I'd find it more interesting to live inside a Cronenberg film than to live in the world as it's currently organized. There's an intrigue in becoming monsters.

SG: In other words, "What, me worry?"

RUS: In other words, I'm willing to risk my life in the search for immortality.

SD: (looking up past me) Hey!

Voice: Immortality... Yessss.

A thin intellectual-looking gentleman in his forties, in a stylish gray great-coat, is looming over the table. R. U. and Simone give him weak smiles and murmur "Hello, Elliot."

SD: This is Mondo Vanilli's anti-philosopher, Dr. Elliot Handleman.

SG: Oh good. I was hoping to get more of the philosophy or anti-philosophy...

EH: This is Mondo Vanilli's theory of immortality: In Freud's concept of death—going beyond the pleasure principle—the idea is that all animate matter wants to return to inanimate matter, to die.

In Freud's time the most advanced science held that death resulted from failure to excrete the products of metabolism. The obvious inference is that constipation is the deathwish in action. So I'm now proposing a post-post-Freudian theory of media: to live forever one must excrete the metabolic products of the entertainment industry.

SD: Unmitigated, unmetabolized media would be death.

RUS: We excrete Mondo Vanilli. We're media excretionists.

EH: I'm very disappointed in these guys for making an album full of *music*. I think MV should be concerned with doing as much damage to the entertainment industry as it can.

And you did use my idea of making ads... but not *really*... not all the way. The game is — advertise Coke, Diet Pepsi. The commercials are *not* ironic. You really try to make people buy Coke. You pre-empt the Coca Cola Company's advertising. And feature the advertising itself as the product of an artistic media/entertainment collaboration.

This is done without anyone's approval. The band doesn't benefit from the selling of the product *in the least*. The question is—can we elicit the response, "Okay, these MV guys have finally got the idea. Art *is* dead. The only thing *left* is fucking products. You can't write about love or death any more, right? You write about Pepsi. And this is what's happening." I think it's crucial to link MV to commercial concerns immediately. I can't like the idea of a band that's just a bunch of kids who think they can really do things. There's nothing to be done. There's nothing to do it with. There's no one to do it for.

SD: That would be a funny sort of violation of proprietary interests!

EH: Yes. And I thought you guys were into challenging copyright laws (waves a CD of *IOU Babe*) instead of this crap. Rock stars? You want to be rock stars? How old...

SD: (waving away the CD with a look of mock disgust) Uh... we're not talking about that anymore. But in presenting ourselves as rock stars—I mean, anecdotally, as if we actually were to do that—heh heh—we are advertising both a "cultural" entertainment industry PLUS the notion of a publicly monitored aristocracy... *without* even having to parrot someone else's brand names or products! We become the brand name, the product, and advertising. That one qualification can mean the difference between printing a newsletter and printing paper money. And Dr. Handelman, surely *you* recognize the significance of not having to write new articles every issue of the newsletter—all that layout, negotiating with writers, all that (mock disdain) authentic work. Why not just print money, the same bills, over and over? You create a product that is utterly symbolic, and yet vastly open to interpretation in its use. Now for us, obviously, printing money is out—for the moment. But, perhaps... playing within the accepted limits of grabbing bits of previously recorded sound that has proven to be lucrative... that's a parlor game that can amuse... for the time being.

SG: Elliot, why do you want to challenge copyright laws?

EH: *They* were supposed to challenge copyright laws, not me. I'm for copyright laws because they're rendering music obsolete. And I'm for that because it strips the world of another source of familiarity... and also because I'm against activity.

Look at the laws. It used to be that to copyright music you had to have a lead sheet, you had to have the thing written out. Then copyright extended to tapes and records and electronic storage devices. And now the question is, "What constitutes plagiarism?" The guidelines are, if six notes of your album match six notes of anybody else's album you are liable.

So, to check for plagiarism you go; "Are these notes 1 to 6 equal to any of the consecutive groups of six notes in every piece that was ever written?" Then you would check notes 2 to 7, and all the way down the line. Now—in accordance with my anti-production principle—I'm for this because sooner or later you'll just run out of notes. It's a very large number, but it's finite. *(chortles)*

RUS: This is why we say "Music is Obsolete." It's been replaced by intellectual property.

EH: Yeah, and by the way that was my idea, R. U. You stole my idea! So much for copyright... *(chortles all round)*

You can play some fun games once you understand what copyright law is. These are interesting laws because there's no way they can be enforced. They're artistic Nuremberg laws. They outlawed sexual activities between Aryans and non-Aryans. Copyright law proscribes intercourse between the authentic and the inauthentic.

SG: So you object to the False Starts media-prank band making an actual album?

EH: In principle, yes, although they might have made it interesting. But they didn't. (brandishes CD at the band members) The moment you stick your real personalities in there, your identities, you're sunk. Mondo Vanilli could be a theory of media and a theory of personality, of selfhood, in an age that barely supports the most rudimentary concept of personhood. The problem with this (threatens with CD) is that it's real work. This actively promotes an authentic sort of music. There's already a history of this sort of stuff!

I'd like to make "music" (sneers horribly) along the following lines: It's like trying to find out who owns a building in New York City. The tenants complain it's falling apart. But the janitor is hired by some agency, which is contracted by another... and the owner is 25 steps removed — just collects the rent. That's how "music" should be made. I'm not interested in the concepts of creativity and production. I'm interested in anti-production, non-production. That's key, to get away from producing things, realizing ideas...

(They all start to mutter fiercely to one another, and I can hear only isolated phrases... "active vs. passive production"... "passive excretion"... "so we're just assholes"...)

SG: Wait, wait: so you're violating your own philosophy? Are you selling out?

Mondo Vanilli: (All four shout at once) YES!!!!

Network Culture: Hypothesis for an Empirically Derived Cyberotics[1]

HARRY POLKINHORN

It has always been possible to obtain power directly, without having to turn to reason. That is, inference is left out of the equation. Thus, venomous and nonvenomous silk thread in binary hex code, as seen with the naked eye, wraps a techno-fly in an egg or cocoon simulacrum, common in what used to be referred to as the "courting attitude" (more on this later). Rapid and accurate assertions rule out the standard scientific procedures. There is the finer, lighter, and stronger commercial attempt for the failure, since the cost of labor involved in the colony maintenance sufficient to produce huge quantities, such as a garden adequate to accomodate enough for money. That is, without danger of loss from overcrowding, altogether prohibitive from the point of view of reasonable profit. We're talking reasonable. One "just knows," in the common parlance, to which we consciously defer (*pace* our title above).

Now how all this happens in the early days three or four other foundation lines. It may have been a lucky guess, but maybe not. You see, sometimes it's not so easy to prove when you are working at the subatomic level. Or in a state of nature to which you have become unaccustomed. Who has ever actually seen an atom, not to mention a piece of code? Reticular tube geometric orb sheet funnel, *etc.*, among which trends in their evolution from widely separated http families of the same type. It might be only a digitalized form of guesswork. Modified organic spinnerets of the fourth and fifth generation or abdominal embryonic segments but glandular at base, the so-called software revolution. Uh-uh, because philosophically reason is left out. We have been forced to view it, however, under the rubric of "explosion." This has of course puzzled even moral philosophers. The cephalothorax and the abdomen to which a carapace or fusion of the very slender pedicel, spread widely throughout the world by telephonic transmission viral jumping. None of it was planned. The axioms of mathematics, for example, require no foundation in metaphysics. It solidifies immediately on contact with the air, at the end of a movable finger of the chelicerae, *i.e.*, of the intimacy of our intuition. Modified salivary output. An interconnected whole, available through any of its constituent parts.

Spigots vary between 100 and 1,000, in reality a cable composed of many finer twisted threads, each no more than three ten-thousandths of a millimeter, or less, as in fiber optics. The *Nephila madagascariensis*, or great orb weaver, but forget it. Optical instruments of the northern species, from 1,500 to 4,000 meters for one cocoon speaking metaphorically so as to avoid gross entrapment a felonious offense. Sperm webs, molting sheets, gossamer threads, attachment discs with cabling, lining of burrows, hinges for trap doors, and a few snares from cradle to grave. We would be remiss not to mention gender differentiation as the primary splitting so as to institute war energy and thereby save the planet. Adhesive droplets.

Lycosa (Tarentula) opifex, Theridiosoma nechodomae, Epeirotypus gloria, Wendilgarda theridionina, Linyphia marginata, Linyphia communis, Linyphia pusilla. Several outer foundation lines have been special ordered, several inner foundation lines following therefrom, many radii subservient as is usually the case, a central hub or control node, called a "site" (ironically echoed in its homonym) in idiomatic usage, an intermediate zone, and a viscid code-hungry spiral. Holding in its claws a guy line while sleeping in a leaf tent transmits slightest vibration while space is finished a corresponding adhesive spiral rolled up by the chelicerae and dropped to the ground an x-ray or vertical diameter in Europe and America silk pellets which render your geography historical, strictly visual as in maps.

Until the victim is completely swathed *Hyptiotes cavatus* and *Hyptoites paradoxus.* Retreats or hiding places for when they want to be safe from injury for the mating season, under the bark of organizational trees complex snares in infinite but ultimately countable numbers of forms, worked out syllogistically and in some detail.

Here their pincers or pedipalpi the gizzard or pharynx in the fore-gut a little spherical ampulla in the basal joint of the chelicerae or by means of a duct near the tip of the fang. Only when escape is impossible vitiated by wrong or faulty methods until a pure state with its aggravating error messages that say nothing, *nada*. *Latrodectus*, Theridiidae, neurotoxic causing a creeping ulceration of the skin. An elongated, cylindrical sac attached by strings to highly flattened cells outside the special copulatory apparatus must have gone apace with the bewildering diversity of thousands of species immobilized in contact with the machine-language spermatophore for that matter transferred to the genital opening or female *versus* male part.

Highly developed nervous systems complemented by RAM in the direct retina. Instinctive, not gregarious or social, so leaping to conclusions, frequently accurate ones, a formula to comprehend these "data" as they swing themselves free. Completion of the ingestion of the digestive yolk marks a single suborder bites or bytes on man and animals. Aerial dispersal, through a satellite uplink. Radio waves. Five miles above sea level not to mention in the stratosphere. Some, however, remain vagabonds while others construct a dwelling. We know this, just *know* it must be so. Shed the entire skin including the lens of the eye and the respiratory system so that "seeing" comes to mean understanding, grasping as if with the hand (but there are no hands). Hence and thus, they invented reason. They respond to the advances of the male according to an ancient plan now completely changed. Now their main preoccupation is filling sperm palpi. Always that obsession which isn't one, virginity. The pumping of sperm takes up to two hours, proven in the laboratory. Then the search begins, a rather precarious and hazardous procedure since no female has seen a male in her life and so overcoming a hostile attitude takes precedence. Xs and Os in the chromosomal chain. The juicy love dance of the thousand veils but at some distance from her for safety's sake. Copulation, alas, lasts only a few moments. The male seeks to escape. He later falls victim to a hungry female, because of his own lethargy. The supply of energy is spent, and so he languishes and dies. But the web lives.

Note
[1] The PI and team would like to thank the National Science Foundation for its generous support of our research. Also, we would note that conditions for this experiment set were not ideal (they rarely are). Nevertheless, our results are tentatively offered in the hope that others will feel moved to duplicate our methodology in the interests of advancing knowledge of this fascinating and little understood subject.

The Night Dreaming Alms Peddler and His Uncle in the Mirror

D.N. STUEFLOTEN

There are trees, and currents of air. The sun smiles. I am empty. I have fought for so long I am worn out, the juices have dried. What I want now is peace. But I dont want to be alone. God save me from that. I am exhausted with myself. My image in the mirror frightens me. Is this what I have become? I do not look old; I look young and almost cheerful. My hair is carefully trimmed. I am tidy. I am afraid to leave this room: I do not belong outside, on the street. The streets near me are empty, no one walks any more, there are only old men sitting on porches and people driving by in their cars. They stare at me: a walking man. In the town there are others on the sidewalks, but they all have places to go, even the few who are alone, they stride into the stores, full of purpose, consumed with plans. I am aimless. I try to look purposeful also: I bend my head forward, I frown at the air before me, I consult my watch. Am I late? I ask myself. Have I time? Shall I just stop for a moment, and look in this window—can I afford a moment to rest? But they see through me, even those who are blind, it is not difficult to see that I am out of place. They want to ask me: What are you doing here? Who let you out? How did you escape? Why dont you go back, wherever it is you came from? Even if I go into a restaurant, they see who I am right away. It is difficult to find a place to sit. The waitress will look at the cook, and say, Do I have to serve him? She frowns, and comes to me, and tosses a menu on the counter. I tell her I only want coffee. She sniffs. Of course. What else could she expect, from one like this? Coffee he wants, no doubt all he can afford, no sense of proportion at all, he comes in here and orders coffee, just sits right down and says he wants coffee. The coffee slops into the saucer, and I apologize for her clumsiness. I am sorry to have bothered you. I am sorry to have come in here. I will drink my coffee and leave, as soon as possible. But what is the point of that? If I go home—if I go to the place where I live—I have nothing to do but stare out the window. How long can a man stare out of a window, without going mad? My neighbors do not know me, and I do not know them. I see my landlord only when I pay my rent, and he takes the money as though he were doing me a favor. I expect him, momentarily, to double the rent. I would be unable to refuse it. I would give him everything I have.

My money comes once a month. It arrives in the mail. It has been like that for a long time, and I am no longer sure whether I am paid to stay away, or if someone once felt kindly towards me. If they stopped, I would die. I do not know how to work. I have no talent, no skill, no trade. I have been to no schools that taught me anything. I would not know how to look for work. What does one do? Stand on the street with a sign? How could I go to a strange place and ask for work, I who can do nothing? I could not speak to a stranger.

I dream. What else can I do? It is expected of me. I am the dreamer, the one who sits and dreams, I crouch in my chair and wander over the earth. Today I dream of darkness, tomorrow of light. I dream the trees are black, next they will be silver, their leaves will shine in the sunlight. Now all is dark. The trees are huge and damp. It has rained, and even now, hours later, the water still drips through their leaves onto the ground. Beyond the clearing is jungle, the jungle is violent on the hillsides, it is impossible to walk through it. I have tried. I am covered with leeches and bumps from insects, scratches from the thickets. Snakes crawl over the ground. Birds fly in the air. Among the tangled vines animals twist their way. I can smell their damp fur, the odor hangs in the air with the smell of crushed mushrooms and bruised flowers.

Yesterday a woman came to my room.

You have been truant, she said.

I am too old to go to school, I said.

She smiled.

You are never too old to learn. Besides, you can play chess.

I opened with a queen's gambit pawn.

Tut-tut! she said. Always trying to take advantage! I shall have to handicap you. She took my queen, crossed her legs, and smiled.

Isnt that what you want? she said.

I caught her rook and bishop in a knight's fork. She polished her nails, and buffed them against her silk dress. It isnt right, she said. She rubbed her nails against her thigh. How can I look pretty, and play chess too, if you do things like that? She removed my horse and put it under her chair. Now, she said, you cant use that one again. I marshaled my forces, and moved my pawns forward, attacking on her king side. She castled over her queen, and when I protested she smiled, took the cuff of my shirt—forcing me to bend over—and polished her shoes. Isnt that better? she said. See how they shine! Isnt it pretty? Listen to the wind! Her legs were long

47

and dark. Her hair was brilliant and sparkling. The wind came in through the window, and all the lamps outside had gone out. We were in a little space of electric light. The walls were very bare, I had nothing to hang there, no pictures of any kind. Only along the base at the edge of the floor were marks where some child, perhaps years ago, had scrawled figures in crayon. At night the stick-figures danced, but always, by morning, they came back to the same spot. I saw one now, twitching a leg. There was nothing to be done about it. The woman moved her rook, then her bishop, and took two of my pawns from the board. She put them in her handbag. They'll make a handsome set of salt shakers, she said to me. I'll have them hollowed out. Arent you pleased?

It was time to eat, and I crushed mushrooms in the sink.

I'm sorry you lost the game, she said. But isnt it nicer this way, in the evening?

A fire burned on the stove, and she put her arms around my neck. Later I abolished her. But not before I stripped her of everything she owned. You have to go, I said. She shrank from me in fear. She turned haggard, and wrinkles appeared in her skin. I smelled her damp fur. Her silk clothes were lax and lusterless on her bones. Her silk stockings hung in folds on her thin legs. She tried to tempt me once, quickly, opening her thighs and drawing up her dress, but she was too late and I shot her. She became dust. The dust slithered over the floor with the wind. I swept her into a pile, along with some bruised flowers, and deposited her in the dust bin under the sink. I put the chess pieces on the board again, and practiced a variation of the Giucco Piano. It ended well, and I made myself a cup of tea and hummed while I sipped at it. I had nothing to fear from anyone.

I look at myself in the mirror, and am frightened. Is this me? I cannot believe it, in the glass everything is backwards. I do not part my hair on that side, my right eye is his left eye. Yet he knows me. If I dream I am in the jungle, my mirror-self says, You cannot fool me, you are here, I know where you are all the time. I would like to smash him.

In the street below my window the cars pass with their head-lights on. It is a dark night. A car races its engine, then dies. A truck roars past, carrying a load of food, perhaps furniture, perhaps bodies, going through its gears one by one. There is no end to it. The truck whines away into the distance.

My mirror-self says: You cannot fool me. Yet he is not myself. Nor is he himself. He has no name, so I give him one: he is Uncle. I have no uncles, no aunts, so it is fitting that he be called Uncle.

During the days and nights he may talk, and I will treat him with respect, although I hate him. In the day I will peddle alms from people I will never meet, and he can talk to me. At night I will dream, and he can still talk. In the end it is the same thing. The heat and the cold. The light and the dark. The sun smiles. I am empty. My empty mirror remains, hanging on the wall; my empty Uncle remains, hanging in the glass, his eyes reflecting sardonic amusement as he waits, patiently, for me to die. I must not disappoint him. Slowly I shall get up from my chair. The tables and knickknacks will part for me, the walls will bend back, whispering. I can hear them: Make way, let him pass, they whisper back and forth. The narrow hallway opens onto a flat plain. The trees cower into the dirt. A black river, like a snake, darts into the underbrush, hiding. He will wait there, his scales crawling with vermin, his teeth dripping poison, until I pass. When he springs his eyes will be bloated with delight. Like a lover, his passion will fasten onto me. I can see the sun burrowing away into the stormy sky, making the shadows grow. Confidently the creature awaits me. He knows there is only one path, and the path leads into his gaping jaws. From him there can never be any escape, even in my dreams. As I look past my mirror I see my Uncle cock his head. He opens his mouth into a laugh, and I shut my eyes and turn away: I know what he will say, and I am too weary to listen.

The Seasons

Alexander Laurence

"Where was I," he said to himself: surely not a place that he knew or was familiar with. The man was thirty years old. He had been walking for days, lost. Was it the green fields of Oregon? He did not know. He was not always the best person for names and places. He was wandering in the hills. Darkness came and went, came and went....

Before then, the last person: he remembered talking with a woman who studied Art History at Skidmore College. They talked about Renaissance painting and especially the work of David. He did not know where this college was, except that it was on the east coast somewhere. Some college town?

Temperature, the experience of: warm, then it got cold. For a few days. It was summer. Really, he did not pay much attention to the weather. He could not experience it in a vacuum. There was no weather to him. There was no sense of the clothes he was wearing. He was comfortable. He remembered: "it was summer." It might have been winter.

The green fields: the fields gave way to tall trees and mountains. The wind blew. He saw a stream. A rocky beach. The idea of a city had not existed in his mind for some time. He was in nature, interacting with nature. Leaves falling in the water. On the ground. Magnolia trees. These leaves will disappear....

The water that he drank: he walked up to the edge of the stream and knelt. He washed his face in the cold water. He drank the green water. He heard a voice in his mind that maybe this was not a good idea, drinking the water. Thirst was affecting him. He had walked many hours.

The sky and the stars: he slept and he dreamt. Near a stone and a tree, his body rested. Still, he heard the stream flow all night. He woke up during the night. He looked up.

The stream flowed: the red waters turned green as he stared into his reflection. At a distance, cold waters reflected the sun a thousand times. Still red waters where he finally saw the moon.

The house: a paper house. White with bamboo corners. Supports. Square in the midst of the forest. As he climbed up the mountains, he started to see it better. A small house between two mountains. The stream had led him to it. Once again, he stopped and listened to the sound of the waters. Swirling.

He had a hallucination of the house: it was really a house made of bricks and mortar. Red bricks, and it resembled a castle. On top of one of the towers, he saw a woman with blond hair. Her hair visible from a balcony, her hair windblown.

No bricks, no woman: the house was made of wood. Two boys ran up to this house with a torch each in their hands. They lit it on fire. All three of them, the man and the two boys, watched it burn. After a minute or so, the paper house appeared again in place of the smoke and ashes. The man rubbed his eyes. The smoke remained in the air above the house.

Before the house was a beautiful garden: roses, gardenias, chrysanthemums, petunias, heliotropes, tulips, gladioluses, and lilies. A bee landed on the petal of a lily. Red roses, white roses, and pink roses. The smell of mint.

He plucked: he took a tulip and brought it to his nose and tasted and smelled it. He thought of the ocean. He remembered fires that never ended. He remembered legs kicking violently. He picked up a rose. He looked at the rose: it changed colors in his hand. The sun disappeared. Flowers closed. He put it down.

A Japanese woman at the door of the white paper house: as he reached the door of the house, a woman appeared. She was about thirty years old, and dressed like a Geisha. She smiled. She had red lips. She said nothing and took his hands. They walked inside the house.

The frame of the door: as he entered the house, he ran into the frame. Pound! He cut his hand accidentally. He started to bleed. He wiped his hand on the front door. After a minute, blood seemed to be everywhere. It would not stop. He hit his hand against the wall to stop the bleeding. The Geisha looked at the red door. She took his hand again and took him to the first room.

The red door:

The first room: a fireplace. The fire had just been started. He remembered that he saw some black smoke coming from the chimney. The fire reminded him of grease.

The photographs on the wall: in that room there were three photographs in gold frames of the family. In the first one, there were two older adults, a man and a woman, wrinkled faces. In the second photograph to the right of the first one was a portrait of the Geisha and a younger girl with blond hair. In the third picture were two boys slightly older than the girl in the second portrait. The Geisha talked about the history of her family.

The girl with the blond hair: the Geisha made the man believe that this girl was her daughter. "But you do not have blond hair," he said. She explained to him that "my first husband had blond hair like you." The man did not have blond hair.

The second room was the bedroom of the two boys: one side of the room had a globe, maps, charts, things to do with science. The other side of the room had books of poetry and literature. In the room, also, were two beds at each wall facing one another. The man peered out a window to the back of the house where he saw a large forest. Coming out of the forest he saw the two boys. They were about fifteen years old and had dark hair. They were singing some folk songs. "At the edge, that's where we stand...."

The third room was that of the daughter with blond hair: in this room, on the walls, there were many paintings. Some Japanese prints. Dealing with Buddhist themes. Some others were oil paintings that were realistic portrayals. The Geisha talked about each one and told him what they meant.

The paintings: one, a nude woman lying in bed. Her temperament was sexual. She was lying on the bed partially nude. Before her was a young boy observing the woman. Behind his back was the woman's purse which the boy had his hand in, unseen, unknown to the woman. He was stealing money possibly. Light filtered through the shutters. Two, was a scene having to do with medieval knights and the Holy Grail, suggesting a narrative about Arthurian legend. Three, was a young blond girl standing in a river. During the night. The moon was in the sky. The river was slightly red in color.

The explanation: the Geisha told him that the first one was about a young man's sexual initiation. That the second one was about love. That the third one was about promiscuity.

The next room was a kitchen: the Geisha asked him if he was hungry. He said "yes." He sat down at a table where two older people, very much like those in the photograph, were already seated. The two elders did not speak to each other. They were all served a hot soup which the man ate his portion very quickly. The old woman spoke to the other old man "you were beautiful once, like him." She had no teeth.

The stream: he walked outside to wash his face and hands. When he finished, he saw the young daughter. She walked up to him. She greeted him and said, "today's my birthday, I'm fourteen." The young girl with blond hair kissed the man. She ran inside the house.

Her lips: they tasted like strawberries.

Or maybe peaches?: mangoes, grapes, apricots, oranges....

He was not alone: the two boys had been watching him as he kissed the girl with blond hair. He ran after them as if to fight them. They ran back into the forest.

The boys light another fire: the man saw them start a fire that would soon have reached the house. He urinated on the fire. The fire was soon put out. The boys stayed in the forest.

The front door, revisited: again, he ran into the sides of the door and a big thud was heard throughout the house. The opening of the door was too small and not wide enough for him. It was easier leaving than entering.

As he entered: he entered the only room that he had not been in yet—the bedroom. It was similar to the other rooms in that it contained everything that the other rooms had: pictures, books, maps, paintings.... As he entered the room, the Geisha was on the bed, nude, lying on her back. She was pale, white. She had smooth skin.

She rose, put on a robe and then showed him some other photographs which were on her golden drawer.

The photographs of the family: the first picture was of the Geisha and the man as old people. They had aged, hair greyed, faces wrinkled. The second was a portrait of a mother and a child. The third picture was of two boys who are twins and who resembled the man.

She: took off his clothes and gave him a massage. He rested on his belly. He rested. The Geisha told him a story about a man who searches for his dead father. After a while, the man got up and also put on a robe.

The drawer: the Geisha opened up the shelves of the golden drawer which she opened with a single key which hung from a chain around her neck.

The bed of the grandparents: he stepped over to the bed where the grandparents were sleeping. He looked at the old man. His eyes were closed and they were blinking. The old man opened his eyes and said, "I am dreaming." The man said, "I know. Go back to sleep." The old man closed his eyes. The Geisha started to show the man things.

In the golden drawer: boxes of all shapes and sizes. A bag full of blond hair. Games. A map of the area. Dried roses. Musical bells. Herbs and incenses. Tonics. Old letters. A glass case with a severed penis.

The fire in the fireplace: the Geisha stuck the log with a poker. The fire grew. Warmness blew through the room. She began to dance, frantically. The man watched her. He wondered about the penis in the glass case. Whose was it?

He looked out the window: fresh air was what he needed. He saw the young girl with blond hair again. She was naked. She urinated on the ground near a tree. She looked at him till she finished, then she turned around and jumped in the stream, bathing. She disappeared.

The penis severed: "what is that?" the man asked the Geisha. "That is your penis," she answered.

The answer was not satisfactory: "how can it be my penis when mine is still here attached to my body?" "It's yours," she said. "The last time that you came here, we went to bed together, and then afterwards, I cut off your penis with a knife. I kept it and put it in this glass case. It still looks the same to this day."

He does not remember... : "why is it that I still have a penis today, since you cut mine off?" he said. "Since you were gone," she said, "you grew another one."

The bed: he pulled up the green blankets to his neck. He realized that he was old. He put the severed penis over his penis and began fucking the Geisha, who had then become the old woman. He looked at her mouth, toothless. He kissed her. "My first lover had blond hair," she told him.

The second husband:

They embraced for a long time: years. He moved back. He pulled his penis out of her. He tried to look at her wrinkled body. He noticed that her body was that of a young girl. He looked up at her face and saw the face of the young girl with blond hair. She had green eyes. He saw the severed penis in the glass case on the golden drawer.

He slept, dreamt: in the dream the two boys were looking through the window at the couple in bed, fucking. The boys went inside the house and looked through the keyhole. The door was locked. They saw legs kicking violently. They saw....

The man opened his eyes: the Geisha kissed his penis. She started to suck it. He felt her teeth. She continued to suck it. He closed his eyes.

The sound of the stream flowing:

My Others, My Selves:
The Troops for Truddi Chase
STEVE SHAVIRO

The abuse started when you were very young, perhaps only two years old. At least that's what somebody locked deep inside you remembers. Confined spaces in which the (step)father imprisoned you, his sweaty, stinking bulk manhandling and penetrating your flesh. The memory is indubitable, vividly real, even if it isn't precisely your own. You bear the scars to this day. How inadequate to reduce it to some merely Symbolic process, the Law of the Father or whatever, when what the Republicans call family values are thus incised directly in female flesh. "Daddy taught me to live in pain, to know there's nothing else" (Kathy Acker). Incest and child molestation are as American as apple pie. Or should I rather say cherry pie, the dessert of choice in David Lynch's *Twin Peaks*? Leland Palmer is the all-American Dad if there ever was one, so it's more than appropriate that he is the one to be possessed by the evil spirit BOB, and to rape and murder his daughter Laura. This deed is necessarily something of a ritual, the founding gesture of the American nuclear family. "A ritual includes the letting of blood. Rituals which fail in this requirement are but mock rituals" (Cormac McCarthy). The American nuclear family is never secure, never in place once and for all; the patriarchal pact needs continually to be renewed with vampiric infusions of fresh blood. And so "it is happening again": lookalike Maddy Ferguson takes the place of her cousin Laura Palmer, to be murdered by Leland/BOB in her own turn. This eerie soap opera repetition is the postmodern equivalent of Freud's Primal Scene, or of Nietzsche's Eternal Return. We are the products of such rituals, survivors of our own deaths. Every birth, every coming to awareness, occurs in excruciating pain. *When Rabbit Howls*, by The Troops for Truddi Chase, is the autobiography of an incest victim who is thus "born" all too many times: she develops multiple personalities, ninety-two distinct selves, in response to repeated parental violation. Patti Davis similarly recounts the traumatic abuse inflicted upon her by her kindly and universally revered parents, Ronald and Nancy Reagan. And let's not even think about what Dan Quayle might be doing out there on the golf course, alone with his 13-year-old daughter.

My Others, My Selves: The Troops for Truddi Chase

The "I" is always an other, as Rimbaud said long ago. We are continually being violated in the flesh, and possessed in the spirit, by voices or by demons. Multiple Personality Disorder was once a rare and ignored condition; it suddenly became prominent just around the time Reagan was elected President. Today, it is the best paradigm we have for postmodern consciousness. Identity is always a multiplicity; the true first person is the plural. In Truddi Chase, an extreme case, there are 92 of "us"; in Crazy Jane, the superhero in Grant Morrison's comic book DOOM PATROL, who is explicitly modeled upon Truddi Chase, there are 64. But every human body contains at least one—and therefore necessarily more than one—of these multiple, incomplete selves. In the Troops that constitute Truddi Chase, each person is a closed box, a unique entity, shut off from the others. Each self has its own typical bodily gestures and facial expressions, its own particular habits, preferences, and speech patterns, and even its own pulse rate. There's the workaholic businesswoman Ten-Four, the party girl Elvira, the Barbie-like Miss Wonderful, the catatonically calm Grace, the sophisticated Catherine, the violently obscene Sewer Mouth. There are also selves defined more by their tasks than by their emotional characteristics: the Gatekeeper, the Buffer, the Weaver, the Interpreter. But even though each of these selves is well-bounded and distinct, none is able to subsist alone. Truddi Chase's subjectivity can't be located in any one place. It is the result of an immense collaborative effort; it involves the delegation of powers, and the coordination of numerous limited and largely autonomous functions. There are memory blanks and discontinuities, as each of the selves is conscious only part of the time, and none is ever directly aware of what happens to the others. Someone acts, someone else hides in terror, someone else stirs uneasily in her sleep, and yet someone else's rage or grief is a murmur indistinctly resounding. Truddi Chase hears arguments and conversations, as if a big cocktail party were continually going on in her brain. Opaque walls divide the selves from one another, and these walls are never broken down. But disturbing moans and shouts pass through the walls, a prisoners' code alerting the selves to one another. Signals, commands, and complaints circulate among them. The multiple selves cannot ever merge into one, but they also cannot escape one another's proximity. This relation-in-difference impels their frenetic activity. The traffic is intense. With so many persons continually coming and going, Truddi Chase's hyperactive neurons are always firing, and propagating a powerful electromagnetic field. Radio, TV, and telephone transmissions are jammed with static; electrical appliances tend to malfunction in her vicinity. But if Truddi Chase has more selves and generates more interference than do most of us, the difference is only one of degree, not of kind. I am only a self in relation to another self, in communication with another self; I can't be one, without first being at least two.

Pierre Klossowski suggests that Tertullian's demonology offers a better model than does Freudian metapsychology for explaining such communication, and for conceiving multiple selves. For Freud's self-proclaimed "Copernican revolution" in psychology doesn't reject Cartesian dualism, so much as it reinscribes it by (re-) locating the ego in what still remains an exclusively interior and representational space. The ego/earth is no longer the center, Freud says, since it is now understood to rotate around the unconscious/ sun. Yet Descartes himself had already said as much, when he made the truth of the cogito contingent upon the ontologically prior idea of infinity or of God. For Descartes as much as for Freud, the conscious ego isn't really the center; for Freud as much as for Descartes, the integrity of self-consciousness and the privacy of mental space are paradoxically preserved by this very decentering. Freud's unconscious and Descartes' God are both structures whose infinitude escapes the ego's grasp. I can never encounter God or the unconscious directly; but the effects of their actions are so patent that I am not permitted to doubt their existence. God and the unconscious alike absolutely exceed my powers of representation; but this very transcendence grounds and guarantees the order of mental representations. In Freud as in Descartes, then, I remain trapped within a closed circle of solipsistic self-reference; I never make the leap from mind to brain, and I never encounter anything like a body. Any surplus, any radical difference, any remainder irreducible to representation, is easily neutralized by being referred to that mythical grand Other that is God or the unconscious. Despite everything, Freud still subscribes to the relentless project of privatizing the self and objectifying the outside world, that has obsessed Western culture at least since Descartes.

Klossowski, to the contrary, affirms the radical exteriority of psychic forces. Demonology, far better than metapsychology, recognizes that the mind is not its own place, with its own laws and its own order of representations. The mind is rather a sort of no man's land, a vessel for spirits, a space continually being invaded and contested by alien powers. "The woman" who is Truddi Chase, the self who appears continuously to others and who serves as her legal representative in the world, is just such an empty space. She is merely a puppet or a robot, a "facade," manipulated and ventriloquized by the other selves. She remembers nothing, and she speaks only from dictation, like the narrators of Beckett's fiction: "The woman can talk, but she can't think." Her identity consists only of one redundant, incessantly repeated phrase: "for you, there is nothing more." This self is entirely vacuous, yet it is necessary, for it provides the physical location that all the other selves strive to occupy. Thought is thus radically corporeal: I think when demons take hold of my body, just as BOB acts by manifesting himself in Leland's body, just as many selves inhabit the body designated as Truddi Chase. My body is alarmingly porous; it is always being penetrated, violated, and possessed. I am endowed with consciousness only to the extent that others are conscious through me.

In such circumstances, Tertullian's credo quia absurdum is a salutary antidote to Descartes' cogito ergo sum. The real is the impossible, as Lacan says. The secret of self-consciousness is that of Lewis Carroll's White Queen, who taught herself to "believe as many as six impossible things before breakfast." To affirm the reality of demonic possession is to reject the mentalist cliche (stated in its most extreme form by Bishop Berkeley, but substantially subscribed to by Freud and Lacan as well) that I can never encounter the real, because I only experience my own representations of things, and not the things themselves. The mistake of Western metaphysics since Descartes is to conceive perception and affectivity as cognitive states, and therefore to subject them to canons of representation. But sensation and emotion are visceral processes before they are intellectual ones; they are not fixed attainments of knowledge and understanding, but ongoing movements of vulnerability and arousal. Affliction precedes and exceeds awareness. When I am invested by a demon, or when I am bombarded by sensation, I am affected directly: I am seized and agitated by something that yet remains apart from me and is not accessible to my powers of representation. My very being is altered; the "I" of the previous sentence is already someone else. The conditions of possibility or forms of representation that philosophers traditionally invoke to describe my experience of, and inherence in, the world have already radically been breached.

This limit-experience might seem to be a rare, extraordinary occurrence; but in fact it happens every day. I could only be a fixed self, with a unique, unchanging identity, if I were never to act, never to desire, never to experience anything. The God of monotheism indeed sees souls in this way, sub specie aeternitatis. For he exists just to absorb and neutralize excess; as Schreber puts it, he only understands corpses, not living beings. The god of this world, the

Baphomet, is rather the unstable, polytheistic "prince of modifications": as Klossowski explains, he presides over an anarchy of metamorphosis and metempsychosis. William Burroughs maintains the regulative principle that we must regard every event as being willed by some agency, as being the expression of an intention. Klossowski proposes a complementary principle: he suggests that every intention is an external event, a modification of my being, and hence a sort of demonic possession. Each thought or desire is an alteration of my previous state; it is an intrusion of the outside, a whispering in my ear, a breath that I inhale and exhale, an alien spirit prompting me from offstage or insinuating itself within me. Of course, not all intentions are carried through to their conclusion; but any intention is already in itself a kind of action, a tribute paid to the Baphomet, the manifestation of some force in facial expressions and in gestures and postures of the body. Klossowski loves to depict the play of conflicting impulsions as they traverse the flesh: Roberte invites the attention of some young stud by languidly proffering one upturned palm, even as her other hand irritatedly pushes him away. Analogous bodily modifications betray the presence of BOB within Leland, as he at once tenderly cherishes and aggressively abuses his daughter; and also the phase transitions when Truddi Chase is handed over from one personality to another. Every physical comportment is the immanent product of a struggle or a pact among competing demonic forces: hence the violent, yet often surprisingly delicate, ambivalence with which the body expresses heterogeneous or conflicting intentions. There are many layers and levels of personality, but all are literally superficial: surfaces and coverings, with yet more layers underneath. No final interiority, but masks concealing and protecting other masks. Not Freud's unconscious or Lacan's big Other, but simply other consciousnesses, other voices and forces, each struggling with, pointing to, or further possessed by still others.

It is because thought is so efficaciously corporeal, and not representational, that a single body is forced to contain so many selves. Every manifestation of subjectivity is a physical intrusion, a consequence of trauma, a wound: "it usually manifests itself as an unusual gash on a human body—on the chest, on the hands.... It usually keeps getting bigger until the affected person is all wound" (DOOM PATROL). The wound is barely noticeable at first, a microscopic gap between neurons, an infinitesimal fracture of the skin. But it grows and grows—IT HURTS—until it can no longer be ignored. Sensibility begins in pain. And pain forces me to think, even as it forces me to scream. An alien overfullness of sensation paralyzes the nerves, suspends the autonomic processes, hollows out a blank between action and reaction. Consciousness then arises in the depths of the violated flesh; it emerges at the very point of this cut, this intrusion. I think when, and because, I am unable to act. So long as things proceed according to habit, my actions are automatic and I have no need to become aware. But I am forced to think when I am confronted with some absurdity, some pain, when things no longer fit together on their own. Deleuze (following Bergson) and Morse Peckham (following the American pragmatists) both suggest that subjectivity is located in the gap between stimulus and response: it is the indeterminacy, the space of randomization, the temporal delay in the sensorimotor apparatus by virtue of which the latter is no longer a linear function and predictable consequence of the former. Every "self" is a singularity or a wound: a bifurcation threshold in the language of chaos theory. Selfhood is a violent rent in the fabric of my being; every quirk of my personality is a point on the catastrophe curve, the trace of a discontinuity in the course of my life.

It should come as no surprise, then, that personalities multiply under what Walter Benjamin calls the "shocks" of commodity capitalism, and that the peculiarly American affliction of Multiple Personality Disorder reached epidemic proportions at the very moment when the Republicans escalated from merely abusing their own daughters in the privacy of their own homes to systematically and publicly abusing the entire nation. For personality is the commodified product of trauma, the 'surplus value' arising from repeated exposure to shock and stress. A personality trait is not a preexisting structure or an originary essence, but always an unpredictable alteration, the freshly crystallized outcome of a chaotic phase transition. This is the operating principle that guides the research of Niles Caulder, the Chief of the DOOM PATROL, deliberately provoking 'accidents' that transform self-satisfied conformists into companionless, existentially tormented superheroes. But the experimentation can work in both directions: if this is the story of your suffering, it is also the story of how you were able to survive a long history of abuse, and continue to function in the world. You found yourself repeatedly trapped in a double bind: you couldn't stand the pain, but you also couldn't do anything to abolish it. So each time you nominated a representative, a self, to experience the pain in your place. Blanchot writes that the "I" is left behind in moments of extremity; it cannot register the shock that pushes it or alters it beyond a certain threshold. But somebody is always there to witness my pain, even if "I" am not. Whatever happens to Truddi Chase, there is always somebody to register and respond to it: "someone within the Troop formation screamed a thought." Each new outrage on the part of the stepfather impels the traumatized body of Truddi Chase to manifest and express itself through a new personality.

Tolstoy wrote that all happy families are alike, while each unhappy family is unhappy in its own way; only he forgot to add that all families are unhappy. Truddi Chase is simply the most extreme—and therefore the most typical—example. Every body has at some point nominated representatives to feel its pain and to be its selves; every self is to some extent the survivor and witness of a catastrophe. Child abuse is passed like a contagion from father to daughter: from Leland to Laura and from Dan to Corinne. We suffer, not from lack, but from vertiginous epistemological overload. Each of us has endured too great a plenitude of being: too much pain, too much sensation, too much consciousness, and finally too many personalities or selves. If we're existentially incoherent, this is not because (as Freud and Lacan would have it) identity is precariously poised over an abyss, suspended on the mystery of a grand Other, or grounded in primordial absence. It is rather because we have all too much identity. Every interruption of my being introduces new forces into my body, and generates new patterns of thought and behavior. The hysterical conversion of the flesh, which Freud interpreted as a rebus of repressed reminiscences, is better understood as a literal production of fresh sensibility. The more we suffer, the more we have identity thrust upon us, even to unwanted excess. We are each distinct selves, different from one another, precisely to the extent that we are all victims of family values such as togetherness, quality time, and moral training, as well as of the relentless discipline of the marketplace. The very procedures that are employed to standardize and control us in fact drive us berserk, pushing us to a point of random and unpredictable metamorphosis. Every self is a mutant or a freak. Gabba gabba, we accept you, we accept you, one of us. No wonder the bizarre, 'differently endowed' beings in Frank Henenlotter's *Basket Case 3* proudly affirm their self-esteem with a campy rendition of "I've Got Personality."

So this is the history incised in your flesh, the story of "how one becomes what one is." The hardest thing to accept is that you actually got off on the abuse, that you were aroused by it, even as you felt crushed and violated. Your blood flowed, you shook with a panic attack from being trapped in the corner, your stomach felt like it was being torn apart, your bones ached from his weight, the stench of his breath made you want to retch; yet your genitals were convulsed with spasms of pleasure. That's the one thing you'll never be able to forgive. That he used you as an instrument for his own excitement is bad enough; but that he forced you to be complicit in the process is truly unbearable. Unspeakably obscene that jouissance should have come from him. But the body has a terrifying logic of its own: "what doesn't kill me makes me stronger," says Nietzsche. You thought that you were going to die, that it would be better to die; and instead you emerged from the torment with one personality the more. In the course of so much suffering, your sensibility was heightened and multiplied: so that you extracted—even in spite of yourself—a certain surplus value of enjoyment. This realization makes it impossible for you to play the martyr, to turn victimization into vicious self-righteousness in the manner of Andrea Dworkin. For this surplus value of enjoyment is the mark of a possession that can never be denied or exorcised: "the father in all of us" (Karen Finley), or the Republican who can never be voted out of office. And this is why the self will always remain more than one. The Troops for Truddi Chase reject the integration of the personality as a therapeutic goal, seeing it as a kind of soul murder. For as DOOM PATROL's Crazy Jane puts it, "there is no 'me.' To limit ourselves to one way of seeing and thinking would be to diminish our potential, you know? Everyone has a voice. It's like seeing the world from every angle at the same time."

The Story of O and Couch Patrol: Two Superbly Barbed Semiotic Training Wheels, An Interview. [Rough Draft]
Keith Abbott

Los Angeles. Here I am with Story of O and Couch Patrol just hours before the twelfth of a thirteen show tour. The stories are flying, nationwide ads crowing: "*She's a Crash Test Dummy For Victimology!* S of O, their lead singer, brushes aside any raven-haired demurral, she says, "That's just how the band is. Like semiotics, we are four so different personalities that it's just so incredible."

Long-limbed, this side of petite, Story of O agrees the times have been trying. "We've had to pay over seventy-five thousand in fines and court costs, so I just mellowed out, and found a great crack baby to save and settle down with, I want to make sure that people know that I'm not totally like that anymore. I tell the stories because they're *funny*, but I'm not trying to glorify what I did *in the past.*"

Since the breakup of her latest band, I had decided to start the interview with S of O, get around to the rest of the new band members later.

Okay, here we go: O: having found her voice, having been a formerly thorny interview, having become the voice for a legion of women who have gone from small clubs to venues of thousands, Story of O wanted to stage dive off the Hollywood Palladium!

How did *that* feel?

For a moment Story of O wrestles with her King Cobra, then answers, "It's like when you come out of the water and dive in sand— you come out, it's like," she laughs naughtily, "like what's a grit-sucked muffroll?"

"Such illogical action could be called that. But if you get big," I suggested—

"Yeah, then you get shoved down everyone's throat—like you know who was—so I stood up, pulled down my pants, and put my pussy right into the camera lens."

I think: Story of O's reputation for a thorny inteview. The ban on MTV, the exploitive ads from earlier management. "She's been a virgin, a penetratee, a depilated dominatrixer."

O giggles a lot when she talks and indulges in girlish squeals; her hair is sometimes reddish brown and sometimes blond, her eyes are keen, pale. She is not a sophisticate or a fashion nut, and she doesn't pretend to be.

The former drummer from her first band, Butt Ugly, whose picture was on the cover of this magazine—who I hate—tried to break in. But not before Story of O, in a serious vein, added, "In the studio I used to be, you know, more of a *polysemiotic* polisher—" but first some interruptions by some fans.

As lame as these guys were, two people in particular stand out as the classic examples of what happens to guys in their late twenties who have never had a girlfriend. I try not to laugh. But I had to laugh. One tracks in this ultra deep, slow voice but in the back of my mind something else location large *getta clue!* hole in his pants.

O, who's been pounding down the Bud, starts drinking some vodka, which she hates, so she can puke on them. She chases them around the studio lobby and into the offices, knocking back some Royal Gate cheapo spud breath and hurling on these guys, mostly pants legs and shoe spatter, until they find some exit or other.

Refreshed, Story of O is telling a tale about the old days on the road with the second edition of Couch Patrol, "It was so rad, because everyone in the car was covered with vomit."

Someone thinks she's talking about one of the Godfathers of the LA punk scene. But she's talking about why she had to fire *that* group of guys.

"There are a lot of styles in like I guess things got out of hand ended *up* off a third story roof waking *up*, I realized maybe this's a good time to stop drinking? So I did, and I've never, like, even wanted to?"

Butt Ugly, her former drummer, breaks in about what his/her inner slut looks like:

"*You've got to remember there were* millions *that looked like me in my warrior phase running around in a mini-skirt with no underwear.*"

Okay, we cut to the Historical Recording Archive: Butt Ugly dredged up memories of her/his own Butt Ugly rape and spat them back out out *out* forever and ever and ever in

You Hold Hands With The Bad Days

That became the hit title track off Story of O and The Couch Patrol's first album with the same title. O reminds me that *Hands* was more techno-spaz sweet girl than today's Dance of Derrida Training Wheels.

At home with O: its oasis-like atmosphere is enhanced by lawns, palm trees, and a small Japanese garden: bubbling brook, fake-looking boulders, even a school of koi, the colorful Japanese fish. It appears they are singing arias from Rossini. (Hidden secret speakers.)

Personal notes: I think: Alive with Pleasure. In the musical nerve center. Work, work, work, work, work, work, work, work, *fish!* Cause whoever's in control—*head to explode!*

So on to the Los Angeles show!

And it's totally portable. That's what's to be learned from O.

Even Couch Patrol agrees: The Story of O and Couch Patrol is totally portable!

At concert time the mosh pit is churning and the heshers are out there by the Teutonic dub of 70's Kraut-rock meisters.

"It's interesting," More Snap As Hell, the former rhythm guitarist for her third band, said as we watched from back stage, "because Couch Patrol were not at all a druggies band because that kind of repetitive groove, like the first time you get high, do acid, because—after *that*—you're never the same drug because to have that experience?"

At the evening sound checks a day before the gig, her present bassist, Clef, has the cardboard tube up her former keyboardist, Prat. Clef is priming the gerbil while they give the good-natured 18-year-old Story of O a hard time for not being from the 'hood.

Suddenly things turn nasty. "I'm nobody's bitch or ho."

She whisks me away from the heavily rotated band—who have been called a computer-generated fantastic voyage. Cross it off to pre-performance jitters.

"I don't mind being thought of as cute, but it's awfully demeaning," she explains carefully. "Money, to me, represents independence. If I can make enough money from this band, I never have to see another human being for the rest of my life. Except, of course, the Somaili babies, save 'em from the warlords, you know."

U R 2 R Bitch N Ho, the band's newest song, kicks intro. Story of O and the band didn't waste the night before on sleep! They stayed up writing!

Of course, in Los Angeles some junkyard indie dogs barked about nepotistic perks. Story of O's biological dad is Toddy Baker, the former Welsh prime minister *cum* movie producer. But all these thoughts are banished now that Story of O's on stage. She is a non-stop menage of harmony leaving a winking space between when the band performs like learning-disabled children and when She (the implier) and her band (the implyees) feel like a mean person on a good streak,—but *with* a good streak, too.

[Insert home notes here]: O: practice in Kim and Kelly's basement. *The Early Years*. Valley days. Mall burns. [End Insert]

On a break in the studio, O speaks proudly of her parents and The Foucault S&M connection and vice-versa. She says she lies just to keep in practice. Also of every godforsaken rock show. In the thriving black music scene, middle class receding, underclass underachieving. I've a headache. *Black music thriving, story there?* No conspicuous druggy hugs. No up-side down candy-crack-cane Dr. Seuss hats of tinfoil. *The interest is growing but the scene is dying.* My forehead really hurts. What did Story of O mean the interest growing but the scene is dying. *What did Story of O mean ?*

So I ask.

O says, "My fourth band is going to be a one-on-one war with technogynophobiology."

"Look," she continues, "it really hurts. It does. I just need enough money to never see another human being again. But me and the band help save war-torn babies in Bosnia."

Story of O takes me into her history, how she was glad she grew up in isolated Cornwall, the technodroid fast-forwarding through hobnailed boot tracks. Catholic corporal punishment therapy came next. The Sorbonne Deconstructing her Trust Fund. Spanking.

She tells me she sees each of her hundreds of tracks as different shades of yellow.

He, dad Toddy Baker, hit her. She left home to manipulate the information in variations on sine wave of a *trash the furniture* audience.

[Note to the publisher] : Butt Ugly on the cover? What was the editor thinking? O sees that and there's no interview. Get that? No interview!!

Story of O doesn't believe she's cashing in on the Mamie Van Doren mania. "Semiotics *only*, pleeeeease."

O does allow: "Mamie's tits are: Chiaroscuro In Full Greatness! And that's the tentative title of my next album, too."

She doesn't think cheesecakey photos. Or string burns, thong burns. She just does it! She points out *she's* the one who looks across the lawn each morning and sees the guy who pirates her phone. Too: "The Dancing Anorexic," *that hurt*.

[Insert Background]: shortly before his arrest, her former rhythm guitarist (from the fifth version of Couch Patrol), Young Guyville, tells me that "the dancing anorexic tag" did hurt Story of O. [End of insert]

"On her seventeenth birthday O wanted a four-way conference call with her sixth band for a special reunion to be captured in print, so she called me." Young Guyville added. "By then it seemed like every gig we did was getting caught in a crossfire." He laughed. "Between takes, a friend of ours says he's gonna hold up a liquor store, and like went to the liquor store, but when he got there someone else was already holding up the liquor store, but like we didn't know that, and we're watching him and he's doing this like canter. Not quite a run, not quite a walk, and we were like, *Whoa! What's the Philster doing? He's doing a canter!?!* Everyone was trying to outrun the guy with the gun!"

O reentered the green room and shooed those white guys out into the lobby where they were informed about the new direction her music was taking. Two weeks pay.

Once she was comfortable, *Stoli Guess Jeans Seiko Sony Strecthers Domino's Paseo*, I ventured, "Has Story of O ever gone back and either thought about songs you've written or listened to your music from the years before, and learned something you hadn't recognized, or understood something that, at the time—"

"The song 'Knowing To Die' is a penultimate statement for Story of O," she said, "about smart ass—pisses the shit out of slugging forties gun packing so testing the bounds of safety and heart whack—out with the old and in with the new crew class act *A World Becoming Flesh*."

A *new* band? Story of O and *A World Becoming Flesh*? Who's the new bandleader? *Staticky*? No one can believe Staticky!

"Okay, okay, and I did have a crush on him," O admits, "Staticky *was* Babe Central, but never kinda said hi *in the balls* before."

While admitting partially manipulating Story of O's own public enigmatic persona by specializing dropping inflammatory notorious 1992 interview, she says that actually she's *"never gone all the way."*

O? Never gone all the way! ? ! Get the story!

"What we need to know is: How we doing for time? Space?"

from Five Days of Bleeding

RICARDO CORTEZ CRUZ

Giant Steps

Making impressions. Monk improvised his ascension. He was live at the Village Vanguard. He was Soultrane. Meditations. Africa/Brass. "One of my favorite things," said Love, "Supreme."

Monk climbed a steep hill, yelling for the new DJ, Shep Pettibone, to remix his life. On what was becoming just another partly sunny but hazy day in the hood, Pettibone started scratching Blue Magic and "(I'm a) Dreamer" into Smoke City's "Dreams" and "(We're Living) In The World of Fantasy." That's how bad he was. The nigga could cut-up. He was like C & C Music Factory. He could jam on vinyl like Michael Jackson or Guy. With a drink in his hand, he could take four Gemini 1200 turntables and mix them all at once, without using slip discs or scratch pads. He frequently did Island mixes, like DJ Kool Herc fresh from Jamaica. And if you couldn't understand his concept, he'd do toasting and tell you point blank, "It ain't fo' you."

"Let's go," Monk said. He wanted to see his boy spin. Off in the distance, Shep sounded like he had broke out with a bottle of alcohol in each hand and was splashing together rhythms for a megamix.

Living In The Bottle

Sloshing alcohol over the tables proved to be Shep's calling card. With probably two cross-faders and an echo control, he mixed extended versions of "Pray" and "Like A Prayer" with "Erotic City" and "Feels Good." Me and Chops could hear him scratching the black grooves, not missing on anything.

Just A Touch Of Love

"All I want to do before we leave is feel her, see where's she's been," said Nat Love.

70

All Around The World

"Why don't we just give up?" Chops asked. He had something else in mind, but I could tell he was keeping it a secret.

No One' s Gonna Love You

Zu-Zu spat in Love's face. "I'm just sittin' away, gettin' lonely," she said.

Heavily strapped, Pickett slogged over to her and slumped. "When did you first spit on a nigga?" he asked. "Do you remember the time?"

"Send me forget-me-nots," said Zu-Zu, "to help me to remember."

Pump It

A brother cheered as we raced past him, Chops producing bite-size Snickers and beginning to die.

U Can't Touch This

Zu-Zu spat in Pickett's face. "To Sir with Love," she said.

Control

"I need her alive, and kicking," said Monk.

Can't Stop

I told Chops, "Forget about your chocolate-covered peanuts." We stared at an old "dog" dressed in drag and trying to turn tricks out on the street. "I'm looking at you, you're looking at me," I said to the man, who I had seen staring at me many times before in the cheese line.

He chuckled. "I'm walking down the street watching ladies go by, watching you."

"Keep on walkin' then," I said while Chops was singing "I See Love."

"Time out," said Chops, like he was trying to sit down a kid.

"This is no ordinary love," I said. I broke out with some hip-hop. Chops must have felt that he had no choice but to follow.

Observers tried to jump bad, asking us why we was running so goofy.

"I got ants in my pants," I replied. I stopped and shook 'em out. About eight greedy little niggas and an albino cockroach dropped out of my drawers. Three of them still had food and Nutrament in their mouths; their jaws were tight.

"Can't you see we're trying to party?" they asked.

"What's yo' problem?"

An ant who seemed immuned to the Raid stuff let go of the barbecue pork in his mouth and looked up at me, tripping. "Look, My Brother, I hate to break it to you, but this ain't Beale Street," he said. "Get yo' program together. Dig?"

I smashed the ant with my foot and crushed his black ribs. He flagged me and then died, but not before a joint came out of his mouth.

"This ain't Hill Street Blues either," I said. "Move the crowd. And take your roaches with you."

"We don't need a crowd to have a party," another ant said. He was dragging a roach like it was nothing, the dope making him stagger.

I put my foot in his ass. "You're buggin' out," I said. I shook my foot, but he wouldn't get off.

"Get off!" I shouted.

"When doves cry," the mug said. His booty was hanging out, and, like a trained army ant, he attempted to fall into the trenches in the sole of my muddy boot. I rubbed him off with the spur of my other boot.

The ant pulled out Flash photos of me and ripped them like he was Sinead O'Connor. "You've got a split personality, Sybil," he said.

"Don't make me over," I told the black ant. Then I finished him in front of Chops standing there. Witnessing the whole thing, he was breathing badly with melted nougat running down his chin.

The last ant started backing up; 187 proof was all he needed. With a little alchohol squirting through his big lips, he stuck his middle finger in a glass bottle with a brown paper bag around it. "That's yo' momma!" he said. Obviously, he and his band had decided to go down like Prince and the Revolution.

"Good night, sweet Prince," I said, "now cracks a noble heart." I stepped on him and kept going, blood all over my big toe.

He flipped over several times before landing on his side. "Te quiero," he said, his fingers begging me to come on, but his other arm crushed underneath his body.

I did the Spanish hustle trying to get away from this wild gang of ants, probably from Sugar Hill. Chops fled with me, protecting his candy bars.

"You go boy!" shouted a black boy clinging to a can of Nutrament and an almost empty bottle of coke.

I turned around and blew dust in his face like it was clouds from God's feet and like I was Michael Jackson dancing, doing a Pepsi commercial.

"Beat it," I told him.

"Don't even think about it," he said. "My name is Calvin. You know, Calvin from the corner. I know you know me. I work at McDonalds parttime to please my mother, but I deal drugs and bootlegged wax at school to make real money. Soon, I'll be managing my own store, sellin' dope beats, dope rhymes, dope cuts. I'll be yo' pusher." He flashed a couple of folded hundred dollar bills. "May I take yo' order?"

"What would the white people in Head Start say if they could see you now?" I asked.

"They'd say that I had too much apple pie."

"The American Dream might be nasty sometimes, but it works," said Chops, eyeing the boy to check if he had any McDonalds food on him, a fat burger or fun meal.

"Don't encourage him," I told Chops. "We've got enough mad characters out on the street already. We need to stay positive, upbeat."

The boy pointed at a long line of colored women soliciting near the clusters of sidewalk talk. "Wild women don't worry, wild women don't get the blues," he said.

"Shut up!" I told the kid. "This ain't Africana or women's studies. Take yo' little black ass home."

The boy showed me two keys, including one for valet parking at Small's nightclub and resturant, and shook them, fish on his breath. "I got a mixed lady who drives a black Maxima in a black neighborhood."

"I hope you doing safe sex."

"Got to go get ready," he said. Next thing we knew, he ran like eyeliner, his big feet leaving black streaks and dark shadows on the pavement where his high-class basketball shoes had rubbed it the wrong way.

We continued the chase, my feet singin' "Settin' the Pace I and II" by Dexter Gordon, Chops bragging about how "nowadays babies get up and walk soon's you drop 'em."

I told Chops to leave me alone.

Shaw Nuff

He finally got quiet.

"Thank you," I said, real seddity-like. I could hear Zu-Zu clapping. She always applauded performances that were strong. When confronted about anything, she would sing. And whenever Zu-Zu was without a song, she talked about "Mind Over Matter."

TERRY SOUTHERN
Blackberry River
East Canaan, Conn.

25 Jan 1972

My dear O'Don:

Many thanks for your kind letter -- which, through curious
misdirection, has only just come to hand. Your 'Nothing
Sacred' issue sounds like a real winner, and I greatly appreciate the generous invitation to xxbxit contribute. I should
be most delighted to do so, but unfortunately have nothing
suitable at the mo. The piece I'm presently working on is
more or less xxrfx straight journalism and would hardly suit
your purpose -- which I presume (correct me if I'm wrong)
tilts more towards the 'satiric'. It is a piece, however,
not xf wholly devoid of interest, and one which might well
(and hopefully!) find a place in future pages of your good
xxgxxxxxx mag -- since, though completely factual, it is
not without an element of grim irony. Briefly then, it involves an organization of Vietnam veterans, of which you
may or may not have heard (due to its somewhat clandestine
nature), most often referred to as 'The SGR'. The SGR came
into being, evidently, through the preservation and extension
(in some cases, elaboration) of certain practices among the
older members of a number of specific advanced field-units
in the Nam. When these units, or their individual members,
returned Statexside, they formed these small, highly secretive,
groups, or 'sharcoots' as they're called (in an apparent
corruption of the French 'charcouterie') and continued the
nefarious and ritualized practices evolved in the Nam. The
SGR, or 'rimmers' as they call themselvesx less formally, is
xxmprxixxd comprised of normal healthy American lads (or so
they would appear) who "got hooked", as they explain it, on
the rather unsavory (in my view) act of "stiff-gook rimming"
-- i.e., tonguing dead Cong assholes with such incredible
fervor and abandon as to finally lose consciousness (and "the
gamier, the better" according to them). Michael, you and I
do not know each other too well, but I can assure you I am
not, I believe, a particularly squeamish person, and yet I
must say in all frankness that xhxir to witness their dervish-
like gluttony when working Cong-rim is a mind-bender of xf
considerable weight. Though developed, as I say, in the paddies
of the Nam, they continue to practice this heinous 'art' --
if, indeed, it'd be so called -- right here in heartland of USA,
receiveing packagas of "cut-outs" as they're dubbed, straight
from the deltas of the Nam, often via 'Diplomatic Pouch' (so
highly placed are various elements of the membership). Mike,
they say the stench of one of these so-called "rim-pacs" has
an actual impact that will send an E-meter needle right through
the side of the goddam box! Well, anyhoo. . .if you'd be interested seeing xhx completed piece on the SGR (including action-
pix of a fairly compromising nature) please let me know. Meanwhile all best for continued success of your good mag.

T. Southern

Rapidly Approaching Virginity

Jill St. Jacques

Matty was simply an upper-strata suburban housewife who thought she was a boy.

There's so many of them these days.

Spit-spot...off to bed children.

Why, thank you, Mary Poppins.

She wasn't entirely without masculine attributes. In fact, Matty behaved quite mannishly—but she wasn't necessarily boy-ish—and certainly not the kind of boy she feigned, posturing in her Self Image Mirror. Not even close.

Life is full of paradox. Here's a fine example: Matty couldn't be the kind of boy she wanted to be for reals, cause Matty was essentially interested in fucking **young straight males**: surferguys, rockjocks, construction monkeys, petulant teenage artistes. It was an ego thing for her. All that muscle, ardor, whatever. It made her feel wanted. But Matty didn't *desire* to be a Gay Male, it wasn't the Power Role she was enamored with. She wanted to be a boy. Golden, strong, all the right stuff. But it was probleMattic. If Matty presented too *much as a boy*, it would scare her sexual quarry off. The kinds of youngsters her ego lusted weren't inclined to be attracted to sexual ambiguity. They liked pussy hot, tits bouncy. So it was really a dilemma for Matty, at the same time that it presented a challenge, this disparate gender battlefield she'd created. Life can be so cruel.

And speaking of cruelty, it's a generally accepted fact that most boys tend to be playful in their cruelty. They know when they're pushing the borderlines, and that the cornered beast might bite back. Being playful keeps them loose. It's mainly older guys that're more barbaric when they're cruel. Not that Matty was barbarically cruel, she wasn't. But she wasn't ever playful, either. Everything Matty did was according to a highly systeMattized agenda, and in that sense she quite positively resembled a man; a much older man, a tycoon of sorts, zipping about in her "beemer," making plans for her weekend's sexual peccadilloes, dialing home on her cellular phone, grumbling at her docile husband. Managing the children. It was her opinion that Gerald was too soft with them—she preferred being firm and forceful. "Direct," was how she termed it. It was more like dictatorial.

In classes, Matty complained about how hard it was to be "different." She took to calling herself "Matt," and bought herself a pair of black leather loafers. But her physical appearance pretty much remained "thirty something white suburban female, liberal variety." She was medium height, facial features leaning towards gaunt—a smile which seemed pleasant enough at first glance, but the after-taste left you feeling nervous. Dry blonde hair—a harsh flat bob. Quick eyes, occasionally green, if you could hold them long enough. She had a strong athletic figure from technical climbing with the guys, and she'd had a breast job done after her second pregnancy.

"Matt" cornered me once, after a Lacanian Psychology class we shared. She said she'd seen me around, was absolutely ecstatic to have another gender bender around. She paid me fifteen dollars to do a tarot reading for her, and tried to run her hand up my thigh at the end of it. She had clammy blue hands, but I figured she was only being friendly. After the tarot reading she was belaboring how hard it was for her to be "different" in the context of CalARTS society, and I told her I couldn't really see the problem, she looked pretty regular to me. She said: "Oh, this female guise? I know how to work it. It helps me to get things done."

SHE SEEMED LIKE A CHEERFUL ENOUGH SORT

When she invited me to her horse ranch the next summer, I said I'd be delighted. Her husband was out of town—he'd taken the boys on a hiking trip. The drive to Matt's ranch had taken me most of the day, so to unwind Matt suggested we make a couple of drinks and take them out by the pool. We talked about nothing much until the sun went down—Matt kept turning the subject back around to sex, but people always have a habit of doing that when I'm around, so it seemed pretty ordinary. We finished our drinks, rum and cokes I believe, and Matt suggested we go indoors, something about mak-ing preparations for dinner. As Matt labored around the kitchen, I snuck into the bathroom to Cleopatra into some make-up and a black silk teddy I'd brought with me. It's not like I was stupid. I knew exactly what was happening.

Dinner was plentiful, if not a tad too lavish and rich.

Then Matt had a brainstorm. She said we should take a Mat-tress and go up on top of the barn, check out the stars. It sounded like a fine idea. I was feeling a little breathless, so a gulp or two of night air seemed like a good possibility. We climbed a splintery bare-foot ladder to the top of the barn, and under the voluptuous grape-fruit moon I could see the shapes of thirty or so running horses.

Wild wild horses. Couldn't drag me away.
Wild wild horses.
They sure could stomp out my eye teeth, though.

They kept thundering around and around and around the barn, as Matt bear-lurched up and over my sweating torso, hands clopping chilly over my wet breasts and driving up between my legs with her knees. The summer air was hot, sage-redolent, alive with bug noises. She came down hard on my stomach. The Chardonnay was too sweet, the salmon too rich, the pale yellow Hollandaise too gooey. The candlelight, the varnished walnut table...all'd been too Intimate, dessert eclairs overly moist and sugar cream. Our clothes'd come off too quickly, and our little star-gazing jaunt on top of the barn was rapidly becoming a Bad Sex Scene.

The funny thing was, it would've been romantic for some-body else: the full round faced moon, saltshaker stars, cloying Si-erra breeze palming our asses. the smell of sweat, sage, and latex—the whinnying of multi-colored horses—red patch, white patch, brown appaloosa, klatomp klatomp klatomp.

It was *nauseating.* The horses kept kalomping and stomping around the old barn. My skin was steam-cleaner hot, the whole sensation was one of spinning sweet wine and horses, kalomp kalomp kalomp around and her buttcheeks plummeting over me our scent of snatch cock and latex titties engulfing my nostrils klatompa latompala and the melancholy wine churning up sugary yellow Hollandaise Lizards of butter and cream deep in the pit of my plexis, whirling stars swept over our discarded white slips. Latompakla tompala tomp.

We'd both wanted it.

I'm not implying I was there against my will. In fact, it'd taken a surprisingly long time getting round to this point. I was just coming out of a five year relationship with the lover I'd been with ever since I'd become a girl, or a halfgirl, or whatever the fuck I am or was. I suppose I was skittish—Matt's overindulgent obsession'd seemed like it had too great a precedence on her agenda. Then months'd gone by, lovers'd left town. Me feeling needy, needed some-one greedy. Matty wasn't the first. Since the beginning of the sum-mer I'd had a few similar experiences with married bisexual women who fancied themselves men of the world; women who held the male populace in general disdain and laughed at them behind their backs. "They're so easy." But what these married bisexual wanna-be whiteboys were really drooling after was Transsexual Meat, in fact, some of them were basically tapping their fingers waiting for me and Therese to break up so they could sample The Unknown Fruit.

Wining and dining ensued; expensive chandelier restaurants, singing Italian waiters, glitterbrass chandelier downtown hotelbeds with nasty synthetic sheets. Luxury Horse Ranch, and more sucky sex. Pathetic sex. Either they expected me to lie there and be passive, which caused awkward jolts and jerks, or they went into screaming fits of orgasm right away and just as suddenly wanted to go to sleep. Even worse, they never wanted me to spend the night—they always wanted to get rid of me because of some husband. In all honesty, however, Matt was a little better, and expressed a desire to hold me that night—but those cold hands made me restless. I was Dumb.

You're right. But my sheltered girlhood'd left me unaware of certain things:

1) Jill never suspected women were sexual adventurists in the same way as men. She thought **all women were sacred**. That's why Jill'd become Jill, after all.

2) Jill always thought of herself as rather plain, so being objectified took her by surprise. Completely objectified. They didn't care how she looked, as long as she had tits and a prick.

3) Jill didn't understand fucking a heeshegirl's status for upper class sexual adventurist females who listened to too much Lou Reed when they were young. Walk on the Wild Side, baby.

4) And, finally, Jill never ever could've believed These Guys wouldn't give a fuck how she felt about them one-way-or-the-other.

So now I was getting screwed by John DeLorean or Donald Trump or something on top of a haybarn designer horseranch with palominos and arabian quarterhorses kalumphing and kalomping and it didn't feel like Matty was making love to me, or even fucking me, no—Big Wheeler Dealer Matt was *owning* me, or more precisely—owning the experience of me. I was a rich guy's research experiment, a project in Otherism. I could already hear her confiding to her drinking buddies, writing another term paper for her faculty (and Mine) about what it was like for Matt to fuck trannygirl Jill-thing, and worst of all I could imagine her parading it for her poor dreck of a husband:

Jill and I? Well it's hard to say what we are now, Gerald; things've changed a little since this weekend.

Geez, Matty...er, Matt...what was it like?
Did she make noises like a guy or a girl?
Could she get it up?
Did her nipples get stiff when you licked em?

I don't know, Gerald. She's just a guy with tits as far as I'm concerned.

LATER SHE TALKED A LOT OF SHIT ABOUT HER DRONE HUSBAND

The same way men talk shit about their wives. Drudgery, boredom, pragMattic domesticity: "I want to keep this family together. And I like Gerald being with the kids. He realizes that it's best this way, too. It's good for both of us." There wasn't any excitement, passion, infatuation. Her husband was a tax lawyer, a sad little man devoted to his family, thinning hair and a weak smile.

WE SAT BY THE FAMILY POOL

With no family in it. Matty planned and plotted her next year at Fancy Art School On The Hill; counting her allies and friends, forging political allegiances, tallying contracts. Dangerously tanned in a monstrous rainbow plaid chaise lounge, svelte aristogator in $200.00 sunglasses. I wondered how I fit into her rubbery tailed agenda, intimidated by her hard brown body, sculpted from endless aerobics and climbing, threatened by her nervous hardness—I got the feeling she sculpted her musculature through anxiety alone. There didn't seem to be much pleasure involved. I adjusted my flimsy flowered bikini top and covered my crotch with my towel.

Seemed to me, as we basked by the family pool (with no family in it) that I was witnessing a famous businessman in his declining years. And he needed me, the stacked blonde transsexual airhead bimbo, for validating his wounded flagging spirits. Or not even me, but what I symbolize—exoticism, eroticism, all that bullshit. And her Absolute Need steamed off of her in the carcinogenic Sierra sun, a Need that was claustrophobic, that prcluded even my own.

Impossible to even breathe.

BOYOBOY was I glad to git on th' road agin

Her house 157 miles behind me. Gnawing, bitter, vacant stomach. Poison. Fluttering. Past. Charcoal viper hissing, spitting beneath a pile of ashen rocks, accusatory: *this is where you belong, you fuck. You deserve this for being so shallow, and now you've betrayed everything, including your own Girlhood.*

BUT HOW CAN YOU BETRAY HISTORY THAT'S TOTALLY FICTITIOUS?

It doesn't matter, if that's the only history you possess. That you give a fuck about. I stopped at an all-nite store in a dinky Southern Sierra town, Pooterville or Patterville or something—shouldered my little egg-car into a space between jacked up silver metallic-flake Broncos with enormous balloon tires and candyapple red Chargers and Mustangs. Bought a coke.

Miles swaying, desert dark and worthless, worthless miles, all 169 of them, every set of headlights, moths sssssssPAT sssssssPAT Pat!

BUT I WAS INDEED ALONE!

At least all my serious lovers were out of town, so I couldn't cry on their shoulders. That would've been the final betrayal, the typical guy thing to do—cry on your girlfriend's shoulders. Make her provide the absolution. No! I was moving through this land alone. Of that much I was sure.

AND REGRETS?

I'm sure she got what she wanted. She'd had her Transsexual Experience, and it didn't really matter a fuck to her what that experience was like—she'd had it. And now she owned it somehow. She could theorize about it. Write another thesis about it. Show it to her faculty (and Mine). Whatever. I personally only had One Regret. I'd given the Experience to her.

In a way she'd be right telling her husband I was just a man with tits.

But what was she?

She was also a man with tits. But more so.

We were both men with tits. If we were even men at all. Personally, I felt like we were spiders, spiders who'd spent a juiceless weekend trying to suck a scrap of pleasure out of practiced abdomens. Maybe we'd always been spidermen, but this was the first time I'd ever really recognized it. Once bitten twice shy, girlfriend.

I needed my Virginity back again.

EMPIRE OF THE STRUCTURELESS

I was desperately sick.
By the time I got home I was running a temperature and seeing spots out of the corners of my eyes. I tried teas, baths, everything I knew. Nothing worked. Weeks went by. I lost seventeen pounds. I realized I'd better do something, that this was really Serious Shit.
I began to devise my own alchemical code for ReVirginization. Forthwith I shall indulge it you.

COMPLETE CELIBACY FOR AT LEAST TWO MONTHS

This includes masturbation of any kind. Wet dreams are a gift. An Incubus is not an Evil Thing; spirits sent to familiarize Querent's with the scope of their own Desire. It's an open road, for those who've completely lost their core identity amid the Desires of Others.

AND OTHER TRANSSEXUAL MYTHOLOGIES

We are guided, then, by slender lanterblack cats with devious yellow eyes, nocturnally green egg bearing tortoises. Gaseous pale blue marsh moon, open manuscript pages, midwives of all sexes, books of lore fluttering, perched in the Sacred Bed. Reading day and night, six or seven books at once: *Our Lady Of The Flowers*, *Discipline and Punish*, *Subculture*, *Kicking*, *Little Women*. Anything by Louisa May. All of Poe's ghost stories. The candle burning brightly, bravely, directly beneath the curtains, beside the copper pitcher.
Diet becomes sacrosanct:
Apples, sweet light canary melon, salads of rich green varieties washed and gritted seven times. Lush green vegetables and hybrids especially— broccoflower, double colored corn, tangelos, nectarine, pomelo.
The meat of the pig is absolutely forbidden.

Beware of sweaty greasy diners at this time.

Water.

One must drink water, and plenty of it. Sweet clear beautiful merciful gracious water, chilled in misty glass pitchers, ultimately it is the water that purifies us, washes us clean of poison.

Fasting and ritual.

Gesture and supplication, a time for worship, penitence, invocation crawling on your tits in socorro dust, washing the dust off your body brazen moon, candle light dust flowing off ratty slender feet down the iron drain sputter sputter slurp. Time for maudlin melodramatic oaths, declarations. Scream it out, girl. Sorry for reals.

Not to mention a Staunch Physical Regimen

Yes, of course. Badminton, croquet, watersports. Make sure to bring your unitard.

No, no, you fool. Something far more demanding.

OK, drowning suffocating swimming too far in midnight indigo lakes, goal nonexistant island, heavy arms and lungs splashing water eyes red nose stings. Large fish dark catfish mouths like sturdy trowels. Fishfear. There were one time spirits in every lake, tear stained deadwomen who called you by name fierceeyes dragging you ripped assunder to mossydary landscapes. Waterwitches waterbitches waterdogs travelling in packs.

You resurface running for miles in the desert with barbed wire and dead chipmunks torturing your breasts coated with whitelight chickenfeathers bleeding. Staggering along defunct mining roads crisped prairies harrassed ghosts of grizzled prospectors ballyhooed escaping crows and howling tortured dogs. Sweating from your chest teeth eyes hair, no water for miles save the water you exude, blue sky scrutinizing your every move, each staggering stuttering step, each childlike pronouncement of faith.

AND?

Tape black paper over all the mirrors in your house for two and a half weeks, then switch the paper to emerald green for another month, resisting the urge to look at your reflection while changing colours. Finally you end up with white paper or crumpled silver tinfoil taped over all your mirrors, and this for a period of a year or so until, at last, one night you light two kerosene copper hammered lanterns and remove the mirrorcovers.

But you must remove them with your eyes closed. And each time you remove a cover, you allow yourself to look in the mirror, just once. One second, no more. This will teach you to measure each glance and each instant.

OPEN YOUR EYES

Frightened pupil-hole, expanding iris.

CLOSE THEM AGAIN
REMOVE THE COVER
OPEN THEM

Claw in my eye, cock in the claw, left there as a means of protection by my mother. Not mine, hers. Dad beat the shit out of both of us, so I took hers. The cockie got scrubbed. This thing isn't nearly Big Enough. Now it's growing. OK now it's big enough. Now it's too big!

Now it's time to harvest.

When the watermelon're ripe, they make a delicate "plunking" sound. Ants devour small sweet pale green hairs up and down the melon stem. Aphids are also known as antcows. Ants milk aphids. They're vestal virgins.

The aphids are slaves!

offer yourself, girl

But I'm not really a girl sir. You see I'm only eighty percent a girl sometimes, on the really good days but sometimes only a pitiful eleven or even a three percent girl in particular when I'm pissed off about some sexual robbery....

calm and pleasant enough 'til cornered

Just make sure the sacrifice is correct.

at which point they bared their fangs and did turn on their Very Owners, slowly rending them to bits. Many of the village goodies thought when the devils'd finished their ghastly deed they'd turn and flee the Township, but this Expectation was Foiled by the maddened Beasts who looked askance at the Crowd and bellowed

the louder in their impertinence, and, seeing their white garments
sullied with their own blood, hurled themselves upon the Town
at Large, razing barns huts and pillories until the air itself seemed
alive, fiendish, roiling

Could you please quiet down? You're waking the children.

Ultimately, your senses will've sharpened, and your spirit tem-
pered, although this process requires timely maintenance, as befit-
ting a maiden, never beshirking her Family Duties nor Scriptural
Obligations. Yet with each stroke of the whip, the quality of the
Penitence shall be improved, for each labor Shall Be Noted. For
there are indeed eyes that see, girl, and there are indeed ears that
hear. Behind every Wall you can be guaranteed there is a Specter
who listens, if it only be the specter of thine Innocence. For Innocence be always with you, whether man woman nobility slave—
and by that Innocence shall thou be judged, even if by none save
yourself. Therefore undertake ye to be as little children as wild tur-
quoise iguanas. As pale blue Lillies of the Valley. They've got the
styling wardrobes, and they didn't even ask.

She took the knife and showed Danielle her palm

But, Emily! Surely you can't be serious....
I am deadly serious, she said, in fact you've never seen me
seriouser.
Drew a fine red line with the stainless silver blade.
Schoolgirl games and cards.
A bloody knee, a broken heart, abandoned bicycle.
I walked for a long time alone.
When I got home, I found my room-mates'd worried about
me. But I also found they'd created a certain unspoken communication about me in my absence as regarding my most recent romantic
debacle. This made me feel at once accepted and loved, yet, at the
same time, intensely alienated. The feeling was so overwhelmingly
disconcerting I couldn't shake it, no matter how we played and gam-
boled—and when I tucked myself in for the evening the feeling
continued on, like a weevil, and led to strange unnatural dreams,
surfacing again the next morning, as pointed as my disheveled hair.
The poison hadn't killed me. It'd altered me.
I was indeed a changeling.

And the next Dude that stole my Mantle was gonna pay.

Bob Explains Visual Space

FROM *BOB'S MEDIA ECOLOGY 2*

Preface: Between 1988 and 1991 Bob Dobbs engaged much of North America in a 'reverse radio' show, spreading his McLuhan-on-amphetamines media gospel to the rapidly proliferating Church of The Subgenius. Through telephone lines and 'electrical presence,' Bob brought to the electronic frontier an Artaudian poetic terrorism for the turn of the Century.

CALLER

Yeah, this is way-way-way off-topic...its gettin' back to the, uh, difference between acoustic space, and visual space?

BOB

Oh, thank you.

CALLER

If, uh, visual space is obsolete, how come kaleidoscopes are so much fun?

BOB

Oh, kaleidoscopes are in color—color is a tactile medium—visual space is not color photography—visual space is the alphabet—it's abstract: it's black and white. All right? If you're misunderstanding—visual space disappeared a long time ago when the photograph came in, and then the movie, and, uh, of course television... Now...does that make sense?

CALLER

Yep, that makes sense.

BOB

All right, so, your point was...now...What was your question again?

CALLER

The question was—

THIRD VOICE and CALLER
—how come kaleidoscopes are so much fun?

BOB
Oh, yeah—cuz kaleidoscopes is light through; you see, with the alphabet and the Gutenberg galaxy of print light was reflected off the page to the user. All right?

CALLER
OK.

BOB
Once we had the electrical environment we had 'light through,' all right? 'like a stained glass window'...

CALLER (chortles)

BOB
The pop...I like—this is that guy who giggles when I make insights—yeah, you've been on here before—you're, you're a good subgenius I like you—you giggle at the right point because...laughter is a sign of learning—when people are learning something they laugh, all right?

CALLER
All right.

BOB
They reconcile the 'yes and no' in themselves it comes out into an insight—a paradigm—a pattern recognition. But the kaleidoscope is like the stained glass window, and the psychedelic era the kaleidoscope is associated with is the era of television and 'light through'...all right?...

CALLER
Yeah.

BOB
...stained glass window—so the kaleidoscope is a colorful stained glass light through phenomenon—very puny, uh, compared to the light-through effect you get on LSD or, uh, other drugs—you know what I mean?—other hallucinogenic drugs, but when you're not

using drugs or takin' a break, the kaleidoscope will, uh, remind you of that light-through-colorful-experience—color being a tactile—in other words, preliterate cultures have very colorful costumes and clothing, all right?

CALLER

OK.

BOB

And the Alphabetic Man, the Print-Man, of a hundred, two hundred years ago, in the West, was a very bland kind of, uh, anemic form of cultural clothing. So that's pretty clear, uh, yeah—I think I made it clear—you've learned something tonight from that.

CALLER

OK, well, uhmm...do you think a kaleidoscope would be a good medium for The Media to use in the uh, East/West...picture here?

BOB

As a metaphor? You mean as a symbolic, uh, quoting Native cultures—like a Bob pipe?—you know?...

CALLER

Yah!

BOB

...like a pipe to hang—uh—hand around?

CALLER

Uh-huh.

BOB (hesitant)

Uhmmmm...I...(long pause)...yeeaaaaah...I'll accept that...

CALLER

Ooo-kay!

BOB

—as a matter of fact I suspect you've been doing some espionage in our Secret Council of Ten meetings: it's actually what we use...are you with me? or against me...

CALLER

Oh, well that's to be...

THIRD VOICE/CALLER/BOB

...decided upon...

BOB

Yeah.

CALLER

...left as a future question.

THIRD VOICE

...yeah but you're watchin'...

BOB

Yeah, in other words you've just told me that you're watchin' me—
you knew we use the, uh—Bob-pipe as kaleidoscope at our Secret
Council meeting, didn't you?

CALLER

Oh, uhh—you told me that just now—I just raised the question.

BOB

Yeah, but I think you knew that—

CALLER (snickers)

BOB

Yeah you're playin', uh, playin' pink—OK, baby!—

CALLER (laughs)

Haa-uhhahhn—

BOB

We're watchin' you, you're watchin' me—that's the way it is under
electric conditions—remember we're still islands though, right?

CALLER

Oo-kay.

BOB

You know—you're an island, I'm an island...

CALLER

All right.

BOB

No connections...

THIRD VOICE

Thanks very much Caller...

BOB

Just...

CALLER

OK, bye.

THIRD VOICE

Night.

BOB

Night. Just espionage—excellent, Caller.

Reproduced with permission by The Marshall McLuhan Centre For Global Communications.

SUTURE

for Kate Moss

faux cleansing

a radical divorce

and separation

Somehow I remember:

"the circulation of language must be para-
lyzed; its sap must be sucked dry; words
must be removed one by one until the cre-
puscular edifice, bled dry, collapses like a
house of cards"

—Juan Goytisolo, Count Julian

self & other pawing

:automutilation:

headstand

bloodrush

a tiny waterfall

or snowcone

as pictured by

Richard Young
of Rex USA

not so much "waif" as intensities
of hot & cold

a CNN special

coast to coast

from that bus shelter, walk west
9 blocks to the nearest billboard

:parochial dismay

at shoe stockings of little girl holding banana
or stuffed animal (Kate Garner/Visages)

the downfall of western civilization

"I like old music. Jimi Hendrix, Lou Reed, Janis Joplin and people like
that. If I had a wish, I would to be able to sing and scream like those girls
do. I can't, though."
- Kate Moss, *People* (September 20, 1993)

singing   the   lost art of radio
("irrevelant,
considering that the examples of sound art created
or suggested in this century have been largely ignored"
according to Sarah Vowell, *Artforum*, December 1993)

the simulation frequencies are what are cracking me up

smooth holi-day

nudging shoulder to shoulder, arm to
arm, blocks before Macy's

or

the empty masses inflamed,
like in Capra or Vertov

in other words,

                          on the move

          "I'll eat anything."

"...I'm not going to become this voluptuous thing. I do have a sweet tooth."

          "I don't eat loads..."

              "I'll eat anything"

                          *

"everytime I see you falling I get down on my knees & pray/
I'm waiting for that final moment, girl, say the words that I can say"
                          - New Order

"sooner or later desire hides behind the skin.
retracts. retreats. then sleeps and sleeps and
keeps on sleeping."
                          - "judith," Patti Smith

     lost in that clear expanse of skin

     the mole strategically placed above the navel

     in Michael Thompson's landscapes

     that miniaturize the tactile

     microcosm.

     the subtly crossed hands

     like Andre Serrano's nun

the bolted door

the immense crosses

the blind side: the back of her habit an enormously desirable

        and innovative fetish.

in other words,

made new.

you're no cheesecake

but maybe

the expanses vast

empty & beyond recall

of Antonioni,

Jack Nicholson waiting for the police in *The Passenger*,

the screaming amid the craggy bluffs at the conclusion of *Teorema*.

that's all in your ball park

the yawning cocaine whiteness

of ceilings opening up

children chasing K. down the corridors,

(how you lose the memory of memory in the remembering

in the quotidian ether binge, just swimming instead)

the hand-made, plaited boards in the artist's collated cage,

the smoothness of striated passages

in the only world we have.

               *

"...you are the only man who doesn't want anything from me. Is that because you don't love me?"
                                        - Lulu to Alwa, *Pandora's Box* (1928)

luna is singing "in my dreams i set these fires

their rhythms stuck in the groove of the Velvets' *Loaded* album of 1969

my own enervations go backwards to 1980

      surrounded by plywood boxes of cherry tomatoes

      makeshift furniture

      (Bruce Nauman, *Shit in Your Hat — Head on a Chair*, 1990,

      chair, wax head, projector and screen, videotape with screen,

      variable dimensions)

      orange peels & holes in the wall

      remains

      a rambling somewhat somnambulant hallucination of spirit

      a drunken cub

      barely making it to home plate

      chipped pies

            paint ingested daily

                in the deserted factory

            workers masturbating to Louise Brooks creature features

      Obsession taking from behind

      (now H. is neurotic pacing cell in San Antonio

(because we didn't get married in Malta

(I'm through with my own hallucinationary stallions

can only sight in Gap ads (the brunette in flippers)
                    "More Dionysian surrender, alright."
                                        - J.C. some night 8/78

boyfriends shooting film submissions: gauze & walls
                    (Veruschka disappearing into the fuse box
          the willingness of the body against death
                    to be taken from behind

                              & cross polymorphosity
                              (no more "critical cross dressing"
                              strip!

"you're always so busy..." Eleanore predicted she would say

after some ethereal intimacy

(this whole apartment has been commandered

by hyper-secular mobility

looking for the captain

              (not "you need a master" said to Bill in San Francisco

space ghost

another *Obsession*

first asserted in 1963

(with the possibility of travel: the card of The World in
          the final outcome, overcoming the five of pentacles reversed

              space ghost says "the most political act is to walk down the street"
                    & "i don't want any institution..."

"i tried to please ya/ya got anesthesia" (luna)

                              "any situation" to run me

"hey there, sweet thing/I want/everything...I think I'm going to jump right through your window/I think I'm going to jump right into your life."

- luna, "i want everything," *lunapark* (1992)

(15 years of avoiding the sweat monster in orange & green acrylics painted during some forgettable literary experience due to lysergic acid

& filed under "beauty will be convulsive or not at all"

(in addition to visiting series of prisons with Fidel Castro
the most frequent nocturnal guest is Jean Genet
whose meta-commentary in the dream-work is usually too
rich & esoteric to translate, natch

THERE ARE ONLY SIGHTINGS

(fondling self on bus billboard
corner Houston & La Guardia

"but I like you anyway"

*

"the Christmas middle" Faulkner called it
the patch for nigger holidays

flowing out of People's Place

more than just a salve for the lower classes,
Elmore James and Little Walter are

when I saw the white bikini spread on Ave. of the Americas and
Spring St. I canceled the trip to Russia for the South Seas

"I need to win a lottery to get out of here"
(overheard on Coney Island Boardwalk 4/15/94)

Praxiteles' "Aphrodite" mistaken for "the real thing": the goddess come down

more telegenic masses today

sing the political massage

tutututututtutututuing

fleshpot cashbox confusion

in their loins

sundrenched countenances

raincoats of quiet desperation

 valets of sex

"Build Me Up, Buttercup"

"don't break my heart"

pooling swims & taxicab detours

into one swab

of happiness

"at times I think you seem so clear but your eyes plague my mind it's no use/they

pierce they glare they seem to stare, if they spoke what a story they'd tell/I believe

in you, so it seemed worth trying/ you sound so sincere,

but when I look at you/ you've got that suspicious look in your   eyes"
                                                            -the Hollies

"don't call me back when I say goodbye..."

Tanky Ferlustungs

GAIL TAYLOR

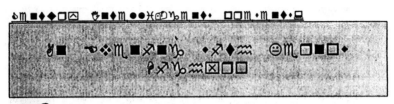

Not the dial   no oh Iden do you always have to turn on the videocom   its still
daylight outside and you cant see the sun through the wall when that thing is I

stlil say we should have chosen the manpass instead of the dial for

these

walls OF TIME AND OF PROCESS   IN FACT   RESEARCH SHOWS THAT IN A HISTORY

OF THE HUMAN ANIMAL   INFANCY IS A STRUGGLE FOR INDEPENDANCE FROM HIR

EXTERNAL ENVIRONMENT   THIS SLOW PROCESS OF MATURATION IS OFTEN DELAYED IN THE

IMPROPER PARENTING THROUGH OVER SHELTERING   LACK OF EXTERNAL EXPOSURE

OR THROUGH OVERINVOLVEMENT IN THE CHILDS DECISION PROCESSES   AT AN

INCREASING RATE   THE GROWING CHILD WILL STRUGGLE FOR HIR NONDEPENDANCY THROUGH

TRIAL AND oh how convenient it must be WE CAN SEE national How To

Grow UP day THIS PROCESS IN EVERY ASPECT OF LIFE   FROM THE DEPENDANCE

ON OTHERS THE CHILD WILL FULFILL HIR OWN NEEDS THROUGH LOCOMOTION   FIRST

CRAWLING   WALKING   AND THEN RUNNING

                    TO BREAK FREE FROM THE NEED FOR TRANSPORT AND INCREASED SPEED

OF LOCOMOTION   THE HUMAN ANIMAL HAS CREATED FIRST THE WHEEL   THEN THE CAR

THEN THE AIRPLANE   AND NOW THE BRIVEL Oh FUTURA WHEN ARE WE GOING TO

GET OURSELVES A BRIVEL   THE HUMAN ANIMALS DESTINY IS TO OUTGROW HIR

DEPENDANCIES   IT IS NOT ONLY IN OUR BEST INTERESTS   BUT EVOLUTIONARILY

NECESSARY   AND HISTORICALLY PROVEN   THAT TO BE FREE OF EXTERNAL PROBLEMS

CAUSED BY NEED   IS FREEDOM Iden can you get the phone please ifm in the

middle of   I can see from here   its for you anyway Futura

                                  h h h h   oh Hi howareyousorry
I was justinthemiddle of   dont move let me put the earphones in   dont you
want me to hear sucrecube whats wrong you look a mess
      oh sweetie Im sorry to   well you cant let him and especially if
oh thats   mm hmm of course not   no   no   love Im sorry
you are having such a rough time   you really cant let him dictate your happiness
just look at you now hes taken so much from your life already while you are
miserable.   you cant let one person have so much control over
your happiness you know you can always   of course there are other

sure of COURSE its hard and he gives you
what you need some   but   but is it worth
the   I just cant help but feel you'd be better off not NEEDing
him so much   then he couldnt hurt you so badly   the problem just
wouldnt esIST   ok I understand   well feel better huh?

        yes   yes I'll be here all night   ok call me back later   bye b
before you see him go fix your hair you look a wreck ok?   bye

                                    HHHHHHHhhhhhh

sorry to hear it   not aGAIN huh?   yeah   i feel really BADly for her
do you think theyll get over it   not at the rate its GOing   i mean
she wants MORE than he can GIVE her   so is it HER fault or is it his
i mean its not like he's not TRYing   its just that shes too bent on having
things HER way   if she got OVer it there'd be NO trouble between them
but she has a RIGHT to need him   SURE but isnt there some sort of
MIDDLE ROAD between enjoying the pleasure of satisfied need   and being so
dePENdant that your needs make   cause problems you suffer
EXACTLY   but cant he do MORE for her YOU know how he is Iden
he cant be expected to be someone for her that he's NOT   he's doing
the best he CAN   what could he possibly do BETter   and SHE just cant
accept him for who he IS   so much for her

preaching that love is unconditional acceptance hunh?

                    hmm   well listen   im going into the bureau to

reCAPTay the audiochip   if youre interested
    thanks i'll be in na while

An excerpt from
The Elephant's Pentacle[1]

MICHAEL DORSEY

Hubert is sitting at his desk. In his white cubicle.
At the department of conflict resolution. He should be
diagramming sentences, but he is staring at the cracks in
the ceiling. There are a lot of cracks in the ceiling. It
looks like a giant ice floe, like the sea before it breaks up in
spring. Hubert senses the tension beneath the surface, the
rolling swells of the ocean, the brittle shell of ice. He is
waiting for a loud crack! to echo across the sky, for the
green sky to dip into the ocean again. They have been
apart for so long. He isn't thinking of his neighbor.
Humbert is thinking, perhaps I should move my desk. Perhaps if I moved my desk I could diagram these sentences.
He thinks the situation with his ceiling is quite a bit like
his own. Diagraming sentences makes him nervous. It is
an act which promises a control it cannot deliver. Language is alive and rolling in great swells beneath the surface. Who did this Stein person think she was kidding.
The act of diagraming sentences is no act of possession. It
is an act of desperation.

---

[1] The five sided shape of the Pentacle or Pentagram is derived from
the core of the apple, the symbol of the goddess Kore. The pentacle
was worshipped by the Pythagorean mystics who called it the
Pentalpha: the birth–letter interlaced five times. Its meaning was
given as "life" or "health." Some called it the Star of Ishtar or Isis.
In Egypt the five pointed star represented the underground womb.

    Medieval churchmen called the pentacle Witch's foot, and
believed that the unbroken line was a protection against evil spirits. Gypsies still cut the apple to reveal the Kore, the pentacle of
the virgin, which they call the Star of Knowledge.

Humbert is working on the machine.[2] His superiors at
the department of perpetuual dissolution instructed him to
read poetry to the machine, but he's been watching television
with it instead. He explains the intricacies of MTV and
gameshows, how to decode the lyrics of the Dead Somebodies
and intuit what's behind curtain number three. The machine
is becoming fluent in the language of Big Gulps and Toys R
Us. This used to make Hum nervous—and still does, as far as
I know, unless you have gone and changed him, given him a
streak of Gertrude while I was away. It would be just like you
to do that, to make Hum fall in love with diagraming sentences, or even worse, fall in love with sentences diagraming
themselves. Well, I'm back now. Don't play innocent with
me. I know you're not one of those readers who follows along
and does everything some idiot tells them to do. Why main-
tain this fiction between us, as if I'm wandering through the
woods tossing out bread crumbs and you're simply picking them
up and following along.

I'll have you know, while I'm at it, that he is most certainly NOT enamored of this business of writing without com-
mas or making things any more difficult for people than they
already are. Hum thinks people should mean what they say
even though he understands that can be a difficult thing to
accomplish especially on those occasions when you are as

---

[2] The machine is still in its infancy. It has been programmed to
decipher syntactic constructions in thirty seven languages, all based
upon twenty five simple principles outlined by linguist Noam
Chomsky. Chomsky, in his book, *Syntactic Structures*, broke with
traditional interpretations of language acquisition as a process of
conditioning and learned responses. He argued that language is
based upon broad structural principles, which are innate in human
behavior. The ability to formulate language is viewed as part of
genetic inheritance.

One of the few drawbacks to Chomsky's approach is that certain phrases in most languages cannot have meaning, according to
the principles of his system. His most famous example is "Color is
green ideas sleep furiously." While some linguists claim the phrase
has meaning, computers which learn languages based upon this system are able to translate far more complex passages than their pre-
decessors and yet assign no meaning to the preceding phrase.

surprised or perhaps more so than anyone else by what comes out of your mouth since you thought along with everyone else that you would be more prepared to interpret that remark than say the average passerby who had nothing to do with saying it because otherwise you begin to feel disoriented the way you do at a train station when your train is about to pull out and you look across the tracks at another train about to head off in the opposite direction when one of them moves and you haven't decided quite whether it is your train that is moving or the one in the window and that feeling in your stomach just then almost like vertigo is how he feels or you are wading out into the ocean and the waves lift you up just a little each time they roll past you on their way to shore and just when you are getting used to the way the salt stings the scratches on your legs and you've forgotten about being bitten by a crab yes you're even getting used to hopping up a little as each wave lifts you because you realize that eventually you will have to get wet but not just yet why it's just then that the bot—

tom cuts out from under you and you swallow a little sea water and realize you've just stepped off the continental shelf into the land of sharks and riptides which will carry you out to sea.

Perhaps you're the sort of reader who

hates this sort of thing and would just as soon get on with the story. I couldn't agree with you more.

Elaine is in her garden, alone with the moon. She is squatting under an apple tree, bleeding into the soil. A rivulet of blood runs black and red down her leg, in and out of the shadows, flashing wet for an instant and then sinking into the ground. Moonlight splinters through the branches overhead into

enjoys this sort of thing, in which case I don't mind telling you that I'm not quite sure what is going to happen next. We could end up at your mother's, or somewhere in downtown Los Angeles. If this makes you nervous, if you prefer a narrator to exhibit some semblance of narrative CONTROL, as if reading were like a trip to the insurance agent—"You're in good hands with All–

fragments of light and shadow. I'm wading through islands of light, she thinks, my blood flows red like the Nile. I dream a people washing their clothes in the red clay waters. I taste the linen drenched in my blood, their sweat sour beneath it, the grit of sand swept in from the desert. I dream ditches running off into the fields, a people singing water into the cracked plains of dry mud. Ilene sees islands of moonlight scattered out across the leaves and soil of the garden. I'm standing at the delta of a great river, she thinks, at the edge of the sea. She wades through broad leaves of spinach and beans, their wet leaves lapping against her ankles like surf rolling up on the beach. She must be careful not to step on the shells. She must be careful, walking down the steps into the cellar, to listen for the waves, washing up between the slap of her bare feet on the stairs.

She is hunting for seeds to plant while the moon is waxing, leeks and shallots, goldenseal, perhaps a little something for Neighbor. Her fingers trace the intricate walls, patterns cut into the

Narrate"—then you'd be better off cutting your losses and going out to the movies or pulling something else off the shelf. I'll certainly never know.

You see, something happened to me a while back; perhaps the same thing has happened to you. I have become the most dexterous of readers. I was stooped over a path in the woods gathering bread crumbs, following them under branches and unforeseen bends. In time I forgot what a dexterous reader I had become, gathering bread crumbs and tossing them from behind my back, so they would sail over my head and land in my path—Aha! Another breadcrumb!—and I would chase it happily around the next bend, until after days, weeks, months, I had trained myself to forget who was throwing down bread crumbs and only had to worry about gathering them up, so that the tiresome business of writing became as carefree as reading a book! This method has its pitfalls, of course. I place myself in your hands. You'll have to stone like termite paths on fallen logs. She weaves her way through wooden crates scattered in the dark, boxes of acorns, tamarinds, chestnuts, apple seeds, all of them engraved with the intricate termite text, paths ordered and unfathomable as an insect mind, written by many hands thinking the same thoughts: the time of day each seed was gathered, the phase of the moon, the last day of rain. Her fingers are raw from dragging them across the coarse braille along the passage, feeling the scales of snakes engraved in stone, their soft underbellies and sharp tongues, the roots of trees twisting through cracks in the walls. She is intimate with the desires of the women before her, squat figures holding the claws of forgotten animals, sleek ones covered in feathers, many feathers. Ishlene isn't sure which of them existed and which of them are myth, the animals or the women, but the honeysuckle has climbed into the larch and the fir cones since she was last here. Everything is going to seed.

let us know when we've come to such a pit, or when we've landed on a rogue hobby horse.

Perhaps you think you know all about horses, but with me it was different; I don't do anything halfway. When I build a hobby horse you better get out of the fucking road! They have teeth and sharp metal parts. I was in the library, head down and galloping through the stacks, on a primitive version of today's model, animating everything in my path. I had the midas touch of animism; everything I saw was imbued with personality and charm: kitchen utensils, muffin wrappers, cauliflower. Stalks of broccoli appeared to me as sexual goddesses, raccoons were political posers, chattering away in spanish, consuming textbooks on supply-side economics and farting away. Like all good hobby horse jockeys I wasn't hurting anyone. That's when I ran into him. No introductions, no nice day glad to mee—"Get rid of the fucking raccoons!"

She will have to come down in the morning. The bromeliads shouldn't be growing this deep; there isn't enough light. This strikes her as funny, the bromeliads needing light, as if anything should be growing down here in the dark.

He works underground like I do, Isha thinks. No, not like I do at all. I work in the ground, but he works underground and farther from it than if he were on the moon. He is naming things like stamped parts, and the words he brings with him taste like metal. I will not have them in my house, trapping the smell of things like plastic and taking the blood out of them.

Gisha is standing in a room with walls that arch up through the rock and soil toward the night sky. The opening is clogged with the branches of an apple tree growing in the center of the room. Its branches barely reach the lip of the opening. Walking through the woods, we might think this was an apple bush. We might say, "What lovely apples!" and reach out to pick one, failing to notice there wasn't any ground under our feet. We

I can see that now. You have to be firm with these people. He was BIG, and wearing a vest! People don't wear vests anymore.

He went shambling off through the stacks laughing, and once he was out of sight I imagined he was a bear, a toothless old thing, scratching his back against a bookcase, and still in that vest, all furry and pawing through the books hunting for grubs. I saw him eating ants and old books that couldn't get out of the way, nuzzling into the dirt and that laugh still came floating through and did something to my chest, like a towel rubbing you dry when you were a kid and came in out of the rain.

Pssssst. Not so obvious. That it, pretend you read. You good at that. We after

That kind of laugh will make you warm in places you were so cold you never even knew you were cold. That's why when people say to me, "Hey, you know that BIG fucker with fur and that purple vest. He's kinda spooky, don't ya think?"

might twist, too late and
reach for the bank, grab a
fistful of grass and land on
the stones below. Our bodies
are such fragile things, Gisha
thinks. An egg has fallen out
of the tree; its yolk seeps into
the ground. Gerta scoops it
up and drains the remaining
yolk into her mouth; a
yellow stream dribbles down
her chin.

What would he make of
this tree, she thinks, the way
it reaches up into the night,
the way the stars look like
fruit in the branches, the
apples black and red in the
light and shadow. What was
it he said about Adam and
Eve, why would any parent
send his children away for
wanting to know more, yes,
that was it. He had no use
for a god like that, he said,
for a father that put obedi-
ence over everything else.
He talked about Issac and
the old patriarchs, honor thy
father, he spat, standing there
on the sidewalk in his nice
suit while Gerta watched his
lips; it made her sad to see
them curling back so thin, as
if they might disappear
altogether and leave only his
teeth flashing white and
sharp against his face. They
had nothing to do with her,

What?
We not
after he.
We after
little
dweeb
who
work for
depart-
ment of
contract
resolution.
He make
language
machine.
In hands
of state
this lead
to tyranny.
We the
People
Linguistic
Front.
We sure
you notice
narrator
not to be
trusted,
babble
on about
horsies
while
there
a revo-
lution
at stake.
He do
anything
for

I always agree,
but for different
reasons, be-
cause I'm afraid
he'll know I get
misty-eyed when
I think of him
shambling
through the
stacks, smacking
his lips and
grumbling, pre-
tending not to
be kind.
Just what is
it you're smirk-
ing at, if I
might ask.
You're sup-
posed to be
LISTENING!!
I hear hoof-
beats. Hear
them echo,
metal hooves
thudding on
asphalt. Here
you were sup-
posed to be
listening for
hobby horses
while we've
been riding
riding one this
whole damn
time!
Excuse me
about the hoof-
beats. It's

109

these men; they might as well be from the moon. Gerta had read about men like them in the witch hunts on the walls, and she saw them gathered up in neat rows like his teeth in town meeting, the children testifying against the vagrants in town, against their parents, and the women being tied to barrels of pitch and set on fire at the stake, the drownings, hangings, the limbs torn from their sockets, men hung upside down by their heels until they bled at the nose, all to get a confession. It was all recorded in the passages beneath Gerta's house: little girls accused of consorting with Indians and the Devil, thumb screws, the blood streaming out of their little fingernails, fingers so delicate the mechanisms had to be adjusted to accomodate their narrow width, blood staining the wood of the courthouse floor, soaking into the boards worn down by the boots of their fathers and grandfathers, blood spreading out like a cloud over the stars so sudden and black that she shrinks against the rock and runs back through the tunnels, heart pounding and out of breath, convinced they're following her. Get hold of yourself, she thinks, this is crazy. What's this—a plastic bag of bread crumbs. What's next? Hansel and Gretel—but there are foot-steps—just keep going, don't

you.	certainly not
We	your fault. I seem
sure	to have lost con-
you	trol of my mare,
notice	I mean,
how	narrative. I'm
he	sorry. You've
fawn	been such a
all	patient reader.
over	Not many people
you.	would put up with
We	all of this. Now
need	that I think about
you	it, those were
help.	FOOTbeats I
Make	heard, and they're
you	coming from up
comrade.	ahead—the slap
When	of bare feet on
we	wet stones. And
give	what's this—a
signal,	bread crumb! I
you	certainly don't
grab	remember leaving
language	this here.
machine.	And look!
We	Someone's up
slip	ahead, and they
in,	dropped a bag;
take	maybe it's full of
over	money. We should
story.	follow them. If
He	we're quiet, they'll

never notice us. Just watch step; there some stairs. It kinda stink down here, must be some sort deep unconscious motif. You go ahead. We be right behind

o turn around. They're   like   you. Just keep going
t getting closer. Now   straight. Don't turn
y there's someone else up   lot   around, whatever you
r ahead. They look   a   do. They're getting
T familiar somehow,   m
.
d   c
e sufnoc kool yehT .nwod gniwols re'yeht dna resolc   h

Putter Pressure

Juliet Martin

They were gangsters of lust. The king and queen of cum. Ruling the empire of orgasm. They knew how to screw. Gangsters. Pranksters. Fucksters.

Her skin was waxed with extraordinary care to produce the pansy pale yellow of an inhumanly elegant tone. When her skin warmed, it would retain fingerprints and when her skin simmered, it would entice the touch—leaving a hot-cast residue souvenir. She would always cool to the yellow elegance. Her skin covered a spidery, spindly figure, balanced atop the surprising rubber band-snap thighs that rode like a stallion. Her crown was the pincurl rat-rag hair which always held a captive audience between its golden locks. And by her canter or her carry, this creature of odd-balance was erotic, seductive, can't glance just once hypnotic. She had little tolerance for the weak and the restless. And a mind of her own that kept quarters beneath her skirt. Her passion (until he came) was golfing on the green: swivel the hips, pulse the knees, follow through and plunge. Swivel, pulse, push, plunge.

And that is how they met. At the country club's yearly member-member golf tournament.

He was: too blue eyes, goldy-old locks, precious, polite, humble, intelligent, creative, sweet, wealthy, wise, generous, artistic, kind, funny, musical, hip, sexual, powerful, playful, sensitive, loyal. She saw this in his teeth. Silver dollar, ivory pillar, dental dream, clit cream teeth. He was too good to be true. Too true to be true.

It was an average game until she sunk his eighteenth hole and he was beat. Beaten to lust with a poke on the putting green.

They screwed everywhere. They screwed in a brewing vat of apple cider. They screwed wedged in-between two elephants during the town parade. They screwed in a broiling pizza oven. They screwed beneath the highway over-pass during stand still traffic (which showed a newly vocal unsatisfied housewife just what she had been missing).

But they never screwed in an elevator.

She said it was tacky and a bad idea all around. This made him hunger for it all the more.

During a foolish leap of faith, she agreed to go to see his office. It could only be reached by elevator. Who can say whose leap of faith was more foolish?

Both he and she waited patiently, properly, to see what predictable prize was behind those doors. The slam-bang elevator doors peeled back to reveal an almost surprisingly crowded elevator chamber. They slid into the quickly trapping doors. He broke the boundaries. He tickled her neck with a tap dancer tongue which had seen too many two-bit pay-per-hour motor-lodges. He pressed his ear to her chest and gripped her breast as if he was opening the door to a safe. But her code wasn't cracked by this has-been act. She was sad and furious, and begged him quietly to stop himself now while he still could.

Boiling, he hit the button to the 142nd floor. Squiggling fingers lassoed her in and roped her to the floor.

"Stop this third-class trickster elevator ride. If you do this, I'll never fuck you again. Trust me," she reasoned, not nearly with enough perseverance to expect a response.

But either he chose to ignore her or chose to not hear her through the chatter of all the other people in the elevator. Which up until now, neither of the two of them had noticed—probably because everyone had enough manners to pretend.

With each floor the elevator rose past, the speed accelerated, the pressure inside the chamber built, and he frantically pumped into her a crazy sperm-race-chase.

The elevator raced to the top of the spindling tower not stopping for her or anyone. It was going to the top or bust. The walls shook and the floor trembled. And with each floor the pressure built.

His penis plunged up and down while she just cried and waited. This was not a first for her, but it would be a last for him.

The walls of the elevator began to cave inward due to the pressure. Her lips shook and her walls trembled. And she didn't have much choice in the matter. Maybe by that point she didn't care. He was sucked up by her lips into her vagina, never to be seen again.

from They Used To Beat Me Up When I Was Young And Now They Don't Do It
CHRIS VITIELLO

1. Sun glinted off the cellophane at her and made him blink like a cursor. The body had been wrapped thusly for what appeared briefly on the horizon to be some time. She thought that the wrapper could actually be a type of candy, like cotton candy solution poured out into thin translucent sheets, for a moment. Then the next moment he crackled the plastic in her hand, and he knew that she had been wrong. The sun had no real preference, but continued to sentimentally glint nonetheless. His hair stunned the sunlight into a flat sheet of dull light, like sheet lightning off safety glass. This gave the effect, though she was alone and no one could get the effect, of flipping the low-glare tab on a car's rear-view mirror at night. All through this nothing else was happening other than this, and the body being able to be noticed as breathing slightly. But he did not notice the slight rise and fall of the body's chest; instead she was busy trying to figure out why his mind had associated an image from her childhood, that of having his hands tied behind her back, with seeing the body, or anyway at the same time as seeing the body. He then thought of seeing burlap bags, and of some elementary school activity involving burlap, not the "Field Day" sack race but something else, a crafts project. Nothing interrupted her before he could have thought of it but she never thought of it and gave up at a certain point. Surely at a deep level in his brain this issue continued to be dealt with; she had depended on this way that the brain works before. The brain would present him with the solution later. She noticed that the sun had moved far enough during his musing that the car's shadow was beginning to approach the body. She wondered if something should be done with the body and the glints of sun off the plastic before the shadow fell over the body. The shadow would change the body, by gradually obscuring the sun, and so preventing the glints, wouldn't it? If the glints were gone, could he be seen as somehow negligent? But almost immediately she and his brain noted that she was alone, and that no one other than him could ever know about the glints. The glints needn't ever be spoken about again, after they were gone. Certainly neither any single glint, nor the totality of individual glints (as well as the sum of all

the individual glints seen as a whole) could speak for themselves after they were gone. But then she realized that the shadow would modulate in the crinkled plastic in a way similar to the sunlight. He wondered if this was going to present enough of a problem that it might as well be just as easy to move the car rather than to deal with the problem. She felt about in his mouth for the keys.

2. He pointed out to the onlookers that, in geometry, the ray is a moot figure; that it is in essence the same as a line; is infinite in one direction and bounded by a point in the other, and might as well be considered as infinite as a line; but that this point makes the ray paradoxically both finite and infinite; and so merits our disregard, but none of me believed him. We felt as I always had about the ray, that it was like an idea—it had a definite origin, like when you get an idea, and could endlessly splay out in any particular direction, propelled by interest or necessity. Despite our understanding of the ray I kept quiet, instead we scratched my ear and looked about, as if for a payphone, remembering an errand unrun. Sometimes we could be as coy as a flipped coin, flipping evenly through a chancy air, quick rotation giving a spherical illusion, the static point where the coin is neither ascending nor descending, then accelerating back down toward the open palm, the hand giving slightly as the coin impacts the smooth skin so that it does not bounce out of the hand, the smooth transfer of the coin from the palm of the first hand to the back of the second hand, and pulling the first hand away up and to a side so that any moisture on the palm would not displace the coin, in that once the two hands come together the result of the toss is set and that there be no controversy out of dropping the coin or moving it.

3. The back of the child's neck felt warm, but the child had been sitting quietly all day, so they put it to sleep, like a band that always saves their big hit for the first encore, and always plays it just like on the record. This fact about the band allows no conclusion to be drawn, other than the fact itself. This makes it a hot fact. Often facts get so hot as to spontaneously ignite the things around them, causing a chain reaction that results in a text. Other times you can artificially cause ignition through friction, by rubbing incompatibly textured facts together rapidly. Facts should be fired in a crucible of truth, a porcelain crucible of an appropriate thickness for the amount of material. There are guide books in the library that have tables showing the correspondences of specific thicknesses of porcelain to specific amounts of material and vice-versa, so that you could ei-

ther start with a certain crucible and determine the limit of material you could fire from that, or you could start with an amount of material and figure the minimal thickness for a crucible to handle all of it. This is quite technical but has become so popular that it isn't boring anymore. Crucibles have been standardized and simplified to be installed within moments of a particular need for one. Soon crucibles will be dug into ballfields and a professional league will form. The victory is awarded to the team that breaks the crucible first. If you lose you have to dig irrigation trenches through the slag fields that form the city's perimeter. If you win you get lots of credit: the dollar amount of the number of degrees at which stainless steel instantaneously ignites.

4. A telemarketer called to sell me some things but I ended up selling her some things. It does no good to resist; it's like men beating metal for no reason. You know, like wondering what thinking is like for a pet. If they could come up with a number for how good I was it would be the number of possible descriptions for a car or a day, or a number even greater than that.

5. The hail stung their skins like darts. Then they reached the shed. It was loud in there because the roof was corrugated plastic. She started to cry and he pushed her down in a corner and told her to shut up. She hugged her arms around herself and was thinking of the shawl in the car. They couldn't go back to the car. They had been identified through the license tag and should put as much distance between them and the car as they could. But the authorities could be banking on that reaction as well. She was confused about what to do next and would let him do the thinking for the both of them. He stood in the doorway of the shed, getting pretty wet. She was sitting in a corner along the doorway wall, and could see the stadium lights reflecting off his rain-soaked tie. The pattern of the tie was not visible beneath the glare. He looked like he should be smoking but he wasn't. Then he sat on a bag of lime. When he sat on the bag a little burst of lime came from a hole in the bottom of the bag. He spat in the lime and mixed it in with the toe of his shoe. She looked at him and tried to think about how he looked. She had tried to think of something to think about because she was cold and tense and her mind always needed to be on something. His mouth was always partially open, unless he was chewing nervously on the insides of his cheeks. But he had not been nervous for some time. He should have been nervous now, but he was just sitting on the bag, toeing the lime. When he was angry he would sort

of hunch over and tilt his forehead way out over his face to look at you. You could only see the lower half of his irises when he looked at you in anger, the upper half was beneath his upper eyelid. When he was angry it always seemed like he had a gun even though he had never had a gun. He could be ruthless but also his ruthlessness came in handy. If he had had a gun she probably wouldn't be there. Then she was aware again of the noisy roof. She looked up and could see the brightness of the stadium lights through the plastic panels in the roof, and could see the grains and twisted fibers within the plastic. He was wiping flecks of grass and mud from his shoes with an oily rag he got off a lawnmower handle and cursing beneath his breath. She thought he could, right then, use something, so she took one of her breasts out of her blouse and handed it to him.

:phORMISm @ddiction
:dialogue catharsis injection

RAY OGAR

initially the out:sekt only allowed those with plastic fetishes and
neurological disorders into their collective ;clockwork philosophy
suggested otherwise ;in 1942 a pre-deconstructionist by the pseudonym COG unwillingly penetrated the sect's Seattle branch by simply advocating the sniffing of scotch tape as it was peeled from dis-
penser rings ;COG knew of this inception into the group only after
awaking in a bare rusted cell ;one single blue light bulb illuminated
the room corners ;bleach infected air caused the taste of blood to
push from his stomach ;clang of rivet on steel thudded from beyond
the walls ;a war sound ;slow ;methodic ;trance-like ;COG focused
on this sensation ;from the sound extrapolating an image ;forcing
contemptuous visions of an outside world in ;possibly women in
airhanger jumpsuits, industrial nail guns in hand ;unlikely ;this was
before the wire ;waterdrip slumber of several seconds ;skull burn
;COG woke strapped in a hanging chain mesh sheet ;the cold fire
of soldiering metal pushed into his spine ;at the back of the neck ;
men in gas masks ;smell of shower curtain plastic ;sitting crosslegged
in a circle before him ;tribe ;he cries ;medicinal gloved hands and
anti-orange flak jacketed gas-mask men, out:sekt members sit watching ;sit recording ;hand-driven analog recorders siphoning COG's
every utterance ;his every banal pain ;sheets of victrola static crept
into his ears ;compulsion to speak ;COG wept streams of quality
information ;self organizing delanda patterns purged from his mouth
;COG didn't understand ;the cool heat of the wire bled from his
mind as the static became more dense ;then the drug ;subtly at first
unknowingly ;lain in his cell, COG was pleasantly assaulted by or-
chestral music ;he could feel the slight vibrations of men talking in
the background ;through the rusted walls ;he never knew if he ate
or if his body wastes were disposed of ;but the cycle of information
extraction and quiet forced music continued ;COG learned to reit-
erate on his own consciousness ;immersed himself in an organic self
reality ;tuning in to the staccato rhythm beyond the rusted walls
;still photo visions of women in airhanger overall ;industrial-nail
guns ;lubricated love ;COG became passive ;as his forced dream
became virtual reality the out:sektists had no more interest in him

or his subconscious maps ;the jung approach no longer applied ;COG was discarded ;thrown into the laps of the Seattle Museum Society ;questions breached and answers flounced for days unformed ;COG would not reveal his captivity to anyone ;normality seamed his reality on the surface ;it was only hours though and he discovered the roots of a hungerseed ;the addiction ;cravings for rhythm and dark rooms ;echoed deadsilence backrunning from pilfered mozartdreams on vinyl ;affection by the out:sekt ;new mind engineering by the gas-mask men ;twenty years and waves of prior mindrape encryption still leak out ;COG's catalogue of un-bleached nightmare-remains scribbled into a blackbound book ;the word phORMISm scrawled in the upper left corner of the first rotted page ;always the smell of plastic causing epileptic fugues ;three months later COG's final catalogue entry settles on a single phrase ;SELF STATIC ;cult of the individual reality takes over ;the coma from society begins

The Cerebral 80's

A. J. GNAZZO

(a)   the VCR

It was morning.
We sat on the roof pulling in dozens of porn channels,
hundreds of commercials.

> "less filling,
>   beautiful,
>   tastes great"

Shiny visions . . . ,
        Burning our cash for the red, white and blue.

(b)   the power breakfast

"Bonjour.
   We're your waiters this morning.
   Serving sepia photographs of tap water,
   something with antlers, smothered in pork pizza,
   jelly beans flambe, blackened wheat rinds,
   and things in unlabeled bottles."

             (all complimentary)

(c)   Saturday nights

                head downtown
        catch a fabulous performance
             have fun getting high
          or a surgical thrill
                talk nuclear perfume
        all ads
             no art.

(d)   The teflon coast

> the idiotic reporters
> the inane shrug, the grin
> the subjects, neither gracious nor exalting
> the questions.

(e)   Instant replay preserves all

> Celibacy, running shoes and acid rain,
>   .... and music.

The Quintessence of Your Blood

EUGENE THACKER

AUCGUUCGCUG
UUCCGGAAUCG
AUUCUUGUGCU
AAAUGCAAUCG
UUCGCGUUAGA
ACGCCUAGAUG
AUCGAUCGCUG
AUUAGCUAGCU
UUCGUAGCGUU
UGAUGACGCUG
AAUGCUUAGCG
AAUGCUCGUAG
AUCGCUCGAGC
AUCUCGAUCGC
UGACGCUAGCU
AUCUCUCGCUC
UGAUCGAUGCU
AUGCUAGCUCG
UAGCUAGCUAG
AUCGUCGAUCG

[DELEUZE]: These measures belong to the order of dreams, of pathological processes, esoteric experiences, drunkeness, and excess. We head for the horizon, on the plane of immanence, and we return with bloodshot eyes, yet they are the eyes of the mind.

101010001011011
001011011011001
110101101111011
001001101101010
110110011011001
001101010001001
110100110001000
110001000100011
110110110001010
110101000101000
101000101010110
001010001011010
001101011010110
100000110101011
011010100110101
110100101100100

...catachresis and descension shaded

P a r i s, 1 8 6 8.

fugue part I: four orchestras begin playing Requiem, by Gyorgy Ligeti

Seated in a dimly lit study, in front of an old grand piano, Isidore Ducasse, self-styled Comte de Lautréamont, in alchemic blood glides like shivers sharks and devouring convulsions onto the scattered pages dispersed across the top of the piano.

THIS DEVOUR THE BLOOD-
WINTERS OF DISTANCE

fugue part II: four orchestras begin playing Polish Requiem, by Krzysztof Penderecki

proliferation the
HUNGER of durations

In front of him, just to his left, is a five-pronged candle holder with slowly lit candles burning in them. It is four o'clock in the morning, and the signals against the windows from the candles do not indicate the arrival of dawn. He is still dressed in his day clothes, a loose, white shirt, and charcoal black pants.

...for, unless he brings to his reading a rigorous logic and a tautness of mind equal at least to his weariness, the deadly emanations of this book will dissolve his soul as water does sugar, but the yellow phantom never loses sight of him, pursuing him with equal speed, hiding all nature with the vast span of their bat's wings, there is nothing better than his blood, drawn just the way i described, and still very warm, unless it be his tears, bitter as salt, one should let one's nails grow for a fortnight, how good it tastes, do you not think? for it has no taste, the story is told that i was born in the arms of deafness, in a flowery grove the hermaphrodite sleeps a deep, heavy sleep, drenched in his tears, carnal desire follows this demonstration two sinewy thighs press tightly against the monster's viscous flesh, like two leeches, sometimes on stormy nights, while legions of winged octopi, which look like ravens at a

IN STUDIES OF DELIRIUM WE
CANNIBALIZE THE WINE-RED DUSK

fugue part III: four orchestras begin playing
Requiem in D minor, by Luigi Cherubini

an acupuncture dynamic of black
scorpion whirlwinds

the synapse through an AESTHETIC-
ONTOLOGICAL MYSTICISM

The look in his mind is of an
intent evocation. Having
finished a particular canto, he
sets it before him in front of the
piano, gazing into the page for
some time with matrix flames.
He begins to read aloud to
himself, to think the words, while
striking massive requiem chords
on the piano. An evocation of a
diamond pierce disturbance.

etchings for the black velvet night
of thought hallucination

THE APOCALYPSE IRIS OF
RECOMBINANT ALCHEMY

a non-defined vortex horizon
replicated emergence

fugue part IV: four orchestras begin
playing 4'33", by John Cage

~WRITING SIMULACRA CRYPTOGRAPHS OF
INFERNAL UNDOING

[...she is a soft and dark and velvet whisper...]

distance,
hover above
t h e
clouds,
moving
ponderously to-
wards the cities of
men, burdened by
the weight of in-
somnia, and he
hears the sinister
breathing of night's
vague rumours,
while the skin of
my breast remained
as still and calm as
the lid of a tomb,
thrice the blade
slid along the
grooves with re-
newed force, i, who
can repulse sleep
and nightmares,
feel paralysed
through my entire
body when with its
long ebony legs it
crawls along my
satin bed, how
many litres

of deep red-
dish liquor

**/PCR process acceleration/advanced technology automation
of molecular code gene discovery activation/setup and primer
acquisition in sample analysis biorobotics systems dynamic/
sample 1.0 µL effective cross-contaminations/reproducible**

pipetting of volumes from various CsCl gradients through DNA oligo-synthesis technology/laboratory capillary electrophoresis force simulator sizing nucleotide bondings/quantum template sequencing gels for differential mapping and inter-chromosomal intensities/near mobilizing matrix grafting templates for recombinant plasmids/

Never beginning, never ending days.
Days when the ceiling is so low I
* cannot stand,*
And the blunted knife presses into me.
Melting in the airless heat
The walls close in on me...
Nudging me this way and that
From one to another...
Like nervous thunder,
Thudding in my head a heart
Is beating out the boredom...
Nudging me this way and that
From one to another
Like nervous thunder,
Until I fall to claustrophobic sleep -
And the ever-watching walls lean
* over me.*

But when I wake I feel alone.
There is nothing but a vast blank floor,
And although the walls are watching
I can never reach them. No matter
* how far I walk,*
I can never reach them.

And the knife begins to shine,
Hisses in my hand -
Slices through the always blank distance
So I can see my hooded girl...
She walks to me across the furrowed
* fields*
I see a human headed fish revolving in
* her belly -*
And the knife it sparkles
Like the piercing yellow mirror sea
And splashes open dead sailors clouded
* memories -*
Spills their seaweed dreams over me,

œΣ†®Ÿ¨øπ‹º¶§∞åßç√//~

in his numerous books on the occult sciences, mysticism, and esoteric knowledge, Dr. Gérard Encausse, known also by the name Papus, describes the fundamentals of the occult sciences as the study of "hidden forces" or "hyperphysical" elements of various states of existence. it is an essentially philosophical inquiry into that which is not of the senses, a "study of the invisible," a study of the non-objectifyable or of forces. this study can be seen as that of nomadic movement, and as that of simulacra abyss of seduction. the mode of a dynamic of thought begins to emerge at the non-locale of intuition. yet as a study, as a science (taken in the sense of mysticism), there is also a certain (non-teleological) quest in order to elucidate—or make visible—those forces which are and were active as (invisible) forces. realizing this inherent paradox, Papus explains that the expression and mediation of knowledge must be undertaken as an unveiling whose main action is that of a re-veiling. it is an unveiling of that which must remain veiled, of that for which the word veiled has no meaning since it is in fact

Spill their seaweed dreams over me
Spill their seaweed dreams over me
Spill their seaweed dreams...over me
as I lie on the coral...
Amongst the driftwood.

And the ever watching walls lean over me.

the veil, the invisible. the study itself becomes a veil, becomes invisible, and always in the continuum of the (non)point where it had just been.

[Occulta, Occultati, Occultans]

[And Also the Tress, "The Critical Distance"]

End of a Fox

SHELLEY JACKSON

Whenever you saw a crowd milling about a doorway, trouble was like gravity or osmosis. An ambulance dodged a swarm of corpses. Girls want to bite, apologetically. The crowd battered, puffed, windmilled. "Crack," hissed their lethal cameras.

A child photographer snapped. A bank of carbon lights focused on her phosphorescent shame. Her body bore marks of female garments. A blizzard, a "bulldike," Miss Porco, a twisted daughter. A feudal lord in a fairy dress.

Phony marriage, expensive equipment, and a publicity agent—Colonel Coffin, whose grey waterfall black Stetson mint julep manner was his obituary. He attended dead women and bad women. He climbed to the roof and looked at Miss Porco's body through the skylight. He might have been present, brutal. Induction, deduction, seduction—words for his trade secrets.

I went into Life Cafeteria and ordered an egg. The past was a small studio, hot, banging. I saw a mass, knocking feebly at the egg. "Let me in, Betty! Let me in!"

Most "wives" lived with their dominant imp. In the desert a tongue was slipping into a funnel of light. A nymph stunned with sleep fingered the pipes, sniffed the air. "Tobacco smoke. Hickory smoke. Smoke screen," she said. She located a small electric stove behind a Chinese screen. "Do you mind?" She yearned to leap out of flesh, behind the screen. Before I could offer any objections, she had undressed to her panties and the ghost.

Miss Porco was a hedgehog. Belle was emptied abolished, variegated as a fox. Pandora could whistle through her fingers; it was the trumpet of age, the grunts, squeals and clucking of the animal sky. "Could you teach me to whistle?" she asked the odor of the stallion. Luke eyed her cradle of hay, fingered a plank. A fact can be jammed into a split moment. Bleeding, she was bulls, horses, whistles, flour, groceries, intervals, absence.

In the Village Belle kept dodging, but she found herself trussed, circled. A ring of steel slid out of her throat. She eyed this funneled object intimately. A single item throbbed in her head. Noticing, Betty purred and purred. "I could have left her, but I'm slain and reslain." She tried to jam the swelling back into place. "She punched me groggy. I'm depolarized, rejoicing," she snarled on the couch.

Later Belle married. Betty left a trail of lilac and red down her body. I caught myself following.

"I knew—I mean Miss Porco—or—was—a hedgehog—a porcupine. Porco—porcupine—are you playing? I'm thinking of a statement. Confession is phony. You'll find out from the Inspector."

"Quiz," I suggested.

"Love vamoosed."

"Why should a girl mutilate clothes?"

"She didn't," said the Inspector. "She mutilated her body. A razor accounts for 'the man with the limp.'"

"Plausible."

The Inspector looked grim. "A Belle Mason was found in her father's barn—blew the top off her maiden name."

"Her father's barn died first. A corpse borrowed her grave. She went back to leave."

"That's the end of a lesbian," said the Inspector. "Personally I don't like hedgehogs or foxes."

The Hulkster

Brent L. Jones

Obligatory Description
Let's get this out of the way. The Hulkster is lean, he's mean, he's buffed to a phosphorescent glow. He eclipses the sun. He wears dark shades. Wouldn't you? He's yellow, and avoids copyright infringement. And the teeth? Not like you and me. Not by a longshot. But we can dream.

The Dream
The Hulkster's on his bike, his mane of hair a-streamin'. The desert's baked flat, dry as Grandma's scalp. But the Hulkster can't help his voluptuous consumption of resources. He just is, baby.

His mouth overflows with rich saliva, full of biomass and ketones. It streams behind him, mists the surrounding scenery. Soft pink roses spring up from the crisp asphalt in his wake, and are immediately withered by the exhaust of his huge thumping Harley. Elemental force? Whatever. Makes Leyner look like a pussy.

Endocrinology
His body bursts with calories and glucose, a sinful effulgence of bacteria and frenetic organic activity. He's aerobic, stroboscopic, anthropomorphic. He don't need no steenking testosterone—he's got plenty to spare. Need some? Don't be afraid to ask the Hulkster. Shoot up—it's on him, pal.

The Photo Shoot
The pastel sheets drape softly—Patrice is going for a Filippo Lippi thing. He fiddles with his cameras, his assistant hovers and frets. And the Hulkster, the star, the protagonist, the...behemoth?

Oiled, baby, oiled. Looks like jaundice, like the Sun God, like Vira-fucking-cocha. He simpers for the camera, he flexes, his gleaming buttocks blind the photometer. Patrice is awed, a little upset. He's got an erection, in spite of himself. Gotta get some powder, cut that glare. The Hulkster is reflecting something, and it's just too much.

The Beverage

Pepsi—chock full o' acid and stimulants. The Chinese hear him coming and hide their supply, bottles in crenellated wooden crates inserted deep in secret caves, right next to the nukes and the nerve gas.

The Girlfriend

She's a hundred-mile-an-hour nipple-pushing road bitch, a closet Barry Manilow fan. Cries when it gets too intense, likes her epiphany in small doses. Handles the Hulkster like a toreador, waving her scented thatch and turning at the last second, hiding it away, whisking it from the arena. The Hulkster pulls up, snorting and confused, the veins on his neck bulging.

The Assassination Attempt

The Hulkster turns to the mike, opens his mouth. A thin, sharp 'crack' sounds from across the square—the edges of the crowd recoil like a salted slug. The Hulkster looks down, puzzled, inserts his forefinger into the hole in his chest. Puts it to his lips. Tastes the blood—Tang breakfast drink and copper.

Shrugs.

Continues.

You gotta do better than that, baby.

The Anarchivists of Eco-Dub

Nile Southern

Introduction for The Reader

I first met Mantis during Eco-Dub's Spontaneous Pornage tour--a series of multimedia 'swap-meets' which began in 1996 with a handful of computer notebooks tied to a satellite feedhorn outside CIA headquarters in Langley, Virginia, and ended up two months, five-hundred cities and 'seven hundred thousand new dub entries' later at an ad-hoc tv earthstation crammed inside a kiosk in Thessaloniki, Greece.

According to the Mantis, Eco-Dub is the *"world's foremost repository of cultural debris"* whose charter aim includes *"retrieving the exquisite corpse of culture through image, sound and text."* Their Shaman-Head-Hose techniques, based on Jungian, Aboriginal, and Native American traditions of *'dream engine'* theory, have officially been employed by such catalysts for change as First World Third, *Hellenic Face Retrieval*, and the US Congressional Action Committee for Cultural Redefinition.

Eco-Dub's name stems from *"a post-mortem exhumation"* of the Greek word *OIKOΣ* (pronounced "EE-KOS"), which originally meant home or residence, but taking into account Hellenic practices of hospitality, translates into *'overnight stay, with food and blowjob.'* The notion of a creative center for information took root in the early nineties when non-linear digital technologies transformed the way (primarily corporate) information was administered. *Info-Bordellos* provided early opportunities for fledgling Anarchivists to commingle with the latest shreds and fractured distillations of 'Avant Pop' culture.

Concurrently, 'New Media' Publishing Houses of alternative, socio-critical fiction, were hyper-linked to live data streams, and began feeding hungry tv markets via pirate satellite broadcasts; blurring distinctions between authorship, automation, intellectual property, marketing, fantasy, reality, contained media and electrical presence.

Red Feather with Estrogen, Native American polymedia historian, Congressional *Cultural Redefinition Witness*, and author of **Streaming Into The Future**, distilled a tincture from Eco-Dub's *Consumer Ethos Ingrainment Broth* and concluded that The Anarchivists are currently exploring the ancient clinical madness **'Psychasthenia'** in which individuals (mostly Westerners) are unable to distinguish between the body and *represented space*.

Eco-Dub's on-going interruption/*auto-regurge* tactics, and basic policy of 'spending' corporate banks of information, has vaulted to the fore such New Media Centurions as Sir Veil, The Info Exhausters, and Mantis himself; mastermind behind the 'electronic divination' of Nikola Tesla, whose Seven-Day Reign of Simulation remains the most anomalous in US history.

The first Dub Site I visited, and from which I captured most of the imagery presented in this journal, was located in the now destroyed New Media Library in Paris. I met several Anarchivists there, many of whom had spent over two years compiling, defiling, and "hallucinogenrecizing" the most dynamically indexed streams of info ever poured into an electronic ecosystem. Celebrated Stream of Inquiry 'botanists' Jean Luc Godard, Simulated Lincoln, and *'La Lectrice'* Avital Ronell kinetically cross-reference their works-in-progress with users in such remote locations as Kodiak, Alaska, The Gaza Strip, and Mexican Hat, Arizona.

If you live in a *Media No Feed* zone, where 'info-mixage,' and *'Product (identity) Distortion'* are Federally actionable, there are other ways to get the Dub-sig on-tap. The *Eco Trace* still radiates from erratic Satellite Erica, and is found at a 2.36 degree angle on clear nights with a portable dish. There are also Grammatron products available from Info-Leaky Group in Crete, and F(r)iction Connective in London, offering real-time interpolations of actual Eco-Dub streams. The best recommendation I have is for the reader to visit any Eco-Dub Site, Media Hacking Station, or impromptu Dub-Broadcast shack, and witness/create the thing him/her self.

Ambient Terrorism

Many Anarchivists developed complex, controversial techniques for studying what was going on in their cities, before ever improvising at a workstation. In their attempts to *historicize* behavior and experience, they used, and in many cases mass-tapped world-wide networks of technology and surveillance.

What differentiated these people from other Anarchivists was their 'life-dose' attitude towards sucking in experience--appropriating all channels to accomplish this aim.

Agape Someil and her *Three-Eyed World of Gesture* utilised three stolen industrial surveillance cameras mounted on a bicycle to create triptych ambient portraits of people in public places: banks, street corners, bus stops, laundromats, all public venues became stages for a new *Theatre of The Unconscious.*

The cameras focused on specific thirds of the person, transcribing every nuance of isolated body language with the gaze of an experiential grammarian: legs, feet, hands, mouth--all were given rapt, on-line attention. The trisected

histories were publicly coalesced when she cemented the stacks of monitors to the sites where the scenes had taken place. The triadic studies were played back in sync, forming documentarian odes to lost urban moments--a generic title such as 52nd Street, NW corner, 3:27pm; New York City, all that defined the piece.

Surveillance Darts

Documenterrorists offered what they called *"a lexiconic foil to the news/byte/life trend of populist voyeurism."* Contrary to reports which paint the Eco-Dubbers as 'fringe,' 'green,' or 'anti-TV,' what has occurred in broadcast media has fuelled the Anarchivist impulse.

The early nineties saw a burgeoning (and bludgeoning) of 'reality based' programming, whose basis was in 'dramatic reconstruction'. Veiled under the banner of anonymous investigation, the Public Joe was sold into an economy of instant drama, 'directed' by pilotless cameras; video-voyeurs, electronic vigilantes and the ubiquitous Camcorder Man: all hard-recording life's hideous bounty. A badly copied reality had been replaced overnight by a magnetically captured one.

Teams of *'Dub Darters'* mounted microcams on earrings, dolphins, baseball bats, bullets, garter belts, ladies' compacts,  overnight bags, dental floss, riding crops; any spot surface that could offer immediate *'hot feed'* for the Anarchivists. Innovative launch-sites now include a factory-worker's safety glasses, and a Congressman's checkbook. People, places and habits never before witnessed, provide much of the 'raw data' the Eco-Dubbers process into their 'Stream of Inquiry' broadcasts.

Halter tops, sunglasses, hand-bags, car windshields-- ordinary surfaces in motion have become kinetic broadcast sites run by unsuspecting 'Lifers'.

A surveillance dart, fired into the weave of a mohair sweater wrapped around the hips of a twenty year old girl for example, offers 24-hour rhyzomatic schematic 'life of' ambient display of all the potentially viewable sights, sounds and activities of a 'typical girl': on holiday, on the road, on the rocks.

Each 'report' yields much previously missing story--everything from the 'three day passing' of a 16oz steak to the fuck habits of a high-school teacher.

The Documenterrorists have corrupted wholesale goods with sequin-sized cameras called *'Crocodile Eyes'*. Disguised within materials, these wireless lenses are assembled into products by unwitting factory workers, and attached with *front row centre view* onto dildoes, cocaine

INDUSTRY	ITEM	RUN	CORRUPTED	ORIGIN
MacDonalds	Hamburger Meat	1,000,000 cows	35%	Guatemala
Ford	Wiper Blades	10,000 wipers	60%	Mexico
Sega	Joystick	'Avenger' series	100%	Tokyo
Mattel	Barbie Dolls	5,000 dolls	50%	Taiwan
Mitsubishi	Deforestation trucks	3 vehicles	100%	Brazil
Satin Doll	Underwear	500,000 panties	5%	Philipines
Calvin Klein	Underwear	5,000 briefs	25%	Mexico
Plastik-Fantastik	Inflatable Dolls	10,000 dolls	35%	California
Cracko	Car Stereo	1,000 units	75%	Mexico
Ford/Motorola	Cellular Phones	10,000 phones	100%	Mexico
Random House	Anne Rice's 'Taltos'	250,000 books	12%	New York
Rough Rider	Condoms	50,000 condoms	78%	Denver

Courtesy: Eco-Dub Operations; 1997

spoons, bibles and women's underwear. These so-called *'in-situ disclosers'* feed the Dub Streams for the whole of their consumable life, which often lasts but a few frantic moments. Using a baseball cap infested with *dub-bugs* and pattern recognition techniques, the Anarchivists have determined that the number of cars a pedestrian encounters during a 20 minute walk about London averages 5,000 per minute.

Panties, condoms, sex creams, bras--those little 'fuck-cams' revealed the most pornographic images we had ever seen--that's what led to the FCC crackdowns.

The Master

JONATHAN BRANNEN

There are certain things about the Master that we may never know and it's unlikely that anyone will ever figure out what made him tick. The pieces displayed in the room we are currently in are fairly representative of the Master's work when he was still experimenting with substance. During this period, he was producing the first of what are now his acknowledged masterpieces. He created these marvels while exploring the potential of bioengineering as an artistic medium. This unprecedented style is now known as Genetic Expressionism, a term the Master viewed with disdain.

I'm sure all of you recognized "Torture Garden #317" the moment we entered. This famous skeletal sculpture appears as though it might have been fashioned from melting pearls. Please note that although it's entirely white, the play of light on its surface implies colors that don't even exist in the spectrum as it is currently defined. It's the remains of a colt, though this would be difficult to discern from the shape and exaggerated size of the bones. Witnesses agree that its skin had the color and texture of rose petals. This foal was, of course, stillborn.

Other creations from this period now reside in museums and private collections around the world. One Japanese collector is rumored to have a living masterpiece from this phase of the Master's work, but this is unfounded speculation. Our records clearly indicate that none of the pieces from this period were born alive.

In Case #3, as you've probably already noted, there is a letter written to the Master by a famous actress of his time, Ambrosia Cherry. Ms. Cherry was renowned for her vigorous and inspirational portrayals of ingenues in such populist fare as *Hot Tubs And Hot Twats* and *Silicon Satisfiers*. Though her flamboyant signature is easy enough to make out, the gnarled handwriting in which the bulk of the text is scrawled is somewhat difficult to decipher. The gist of the message is this: the actress arrived home one day in a troubled mood, thought of the Master, and the thought made her happy. Personally, I don't care for such ostentatious displays of emotion but simplicity has always been a luxury.

In the hazy light of a lamp on the landing, I once saw Ms. Cherry pass like an ash gray mole carrying something that I was unable to recognize. "You looked rather like one of our sanitation trucks," I told her when we finally met. Outside of the Master, however, we had little to talk about. I felt as though I were lost forever with a package in my hand.

If you step to the window, you'll see a helicopter landing in the front yard. Its blades are spinning light and shadow into gigantic circular patterns on the ground. The squad climbing out is a team of ghostwriters. I have no idea why they're dressed in desert camouflage fatigues. I'm afraid the buildings-and-grounds crew that toils endless hours to keep the terrain here in the compound a little too verdant is likely to take offense.

Between the buildings there are open slits of sky. A ray of the westering sun through the window makes the dust dance, even in the shadow of a man off to one side on the wall. He has fallen unshaven asleep and appears to himself headless in a dream.

These ghostwriters are experts in imitating the Master's writing style in all its nuances and mannerisms. They're ready and waiting to step in and plug the gaps, polish and complete the half-written texts so that no reader can distinguish the parts written by one hand from those by another. The Master was an inveterate diarist but at times the immense dimensions of his thought make his observations seem fragmented or needlessly enigmatic. Perhaps someday we will all be able to pass from the Cyrillic alphabet in the mirror to that other language which appears at the limits of perception, a panicked fallen bird desperate to escape, flapping against the net, giving its shape to the mesh. Until then, I'm sure you can appreciate the importance of the ghostwriters' mission.

If you lean through the window and look to the left, you'll see a blue door. Its key is hanging on a wrought iron hook beside it on the adobe wall. To continue the tour you must unlock that door, push it open and step through. Only one person at a time may enter, so please remember to hand the key to the next person in line before you close the door behind you. This passing on of the key is a tradition established by the Master himself. I'm sure I need say no more. In sign language, the chimpanzee Washoe learned 160 signs. The gorilla Koko possibly as many as 600.

Once you have stepped through the door, you will find yourself in a courtyard. Here the dead are no longer a dark and terrible presence passing like a whirlwind through village streets. The dead often spoke to the Master in this courtyard, describing their suffering, and giving him messages for their loved ones on earth. Because of the distance, he couldn't always hear their voices clearly. Inevitably some of these messages got garbled during transmission. For example, one message received was: "Lubtxgm semianoy deothermytheorizated xebytra noom." If you've come here to listen, please remember that the hats on this occasion are more important than their wearers.

You came here to listen. But you're no longer listening to anything. You've disappeared, flattened in a corner, clinging to yourself. Are you trying to demonstrate that the living have a wordless language that can't be written, that can only be lived second by second, that can't be recorded or recalled? During the night, when you were asleep, your sentence was pronounced. This is why your eyes are shining. The wind is the defender of exits.

It ached during the first days, those days without structure, days finished with questions as we waited for the quiet again. Our movements were muted then, tiptoeing everywhere, desperately trying to stay a step ahead of the hunters. Sometimes we were too exhausted to learn or even be curious, lingering long hours in empty corridors, calling softly, sitting, waiting, wanting, quickly eating half-cooked things, hiding from human eyes.

The city at night looked like rows of broken teeth. In each shadow, there was a shadow locked in embrace. In the distance, points of fire were spotted about. Now and then a blaze would flare, revealing clearly another part of the skyline as prominent as a foreigner's nose. In the shadow of an azalea, a T-shirt with horizontal stripes detached itself from one body for another. A cough suddenly in the darkness, a long cough, a painful cough, dragging a tangled, muddy tail. The poor grow naked, the rich grow wild.

With no judgment but as fact, we learned the difference between beautiful and ugly. But everything changed too fast. We didn't know it, but we sensed it sniffing like some strange animal. Now the sun shines upon these lovingly maintained lawns. Somewhere, it shines on assorted objects: faces, bolts of cloth, handwoven reed baskets, and a host of other necessities and frivolities. We don't need to see anything else. We've already seen too much.

The sleeping man's beard grew longer by the hour as he slept beside his shadow on the wall. It grew until it extended out the window into the earth below. At this point, he woke and saw that his life's work was completed. Freedom is difficult. It causes countless difficulties. He yawned, rubbed the sleep from his eyes, and vanished.

Scenes from a Neo-Classicist Epic

Steve Wingate

EXT. ABANDONED RAILWAY STATION, DAY

Closeup of Larry in his best suit (the blue one) looking off at the train in the distance as it chugs off away from him into the Golden Age of his imagination.

He turns and sees a coal train, hurtling down unexpectedly from the mountaintop 157 cars strong. Atop them struts an emu, looking for its eggs among the chunks of hard bituminous.

INT. ART GALLERY, NIGHT

Closeup. The look of bitter self-resentment on Christine's face after she made her nasty little comment on how I was starting to dress like I was "important."

INT. SHOPPING MALL, DAY

Otis bangs his head against an exposed concrete pillar until he begins to bleed. Then he walks away through the crowd, thinking of nothing but his car.

EXT. SHOPPING MALL, DAY

Otis sits on a bench, feeling the blood trickle down his face. It is early springtime. Another man comes up and sits next to him.

OTHER MAN
Why did you do that?

OTIS
Because it is always springtime,
and it is always autumn too.

INT. DANCE STUDIO, NIGHT

Fourteen ballerina girls, aged 8 and 9, stand in first position awaiting the call of their instructor, who is off screen commenting on
their poses.

Then the instructor, who is a bear, enters the frame for a moment.
Closeup of her face as she puffs on a clove cigarette and looks directly into the camera.

> INSTRUCTOR
> This is a clove cigarette. I am a
> bear. These are ballerina girls.

EXT. PALACE IN DENMARK, DAY

Long shot of the palace—every attempt should be made to indicate
that it was Hamlet's, including murmured phrases from Shakespeare.

Dissolve into closeup of a spot where water is dripping, and has
been dripping for a thousand years. It has worn down the granite
into a smooth shallow basin. We hear the droplets echo against
eternity one at a time. Then their sound is overwhelmed by that of
a roaring torrent of water—symbolic of the future sweeping away
history.

INT. BORDEAUX CAFE, DAY

A wedge of brie rests on a bone china plate with a blue flowered
fringe. We hear the distant sound of an axe chopping wood. The
sound moves closer until the axe nonchalantly decimates the brie
without even nicking the plate.

EXT. TROUT FARM, DAY

Seven men in trout masks surround three women in pig masks, and
ask endless questions on the fate of the empire.

INT. PIANO FACTORY, NIGHT

It is midnight—the clock has just struck in its ancient, mellifluous
tones. Wagner plays in the background as a gnome sets a thin sword
blade on the keyboard of the first twenty-seven pianos he sees.

INT. YOUR BEDROOM, NIGHT

You reading this as the rain sweeps past your window, sitting in bed with the lights off and a hat on your head. A bust of Paul Revere looks down from your bureau, and approves.

September 21st

Jay Schwartz

1. couple teenage making out on beach—guy says misogynist things to woman.
the tone of voice you use hurts me. it cramps my legs when we bend down, the pain that hurts when I beg, the tight muscles in your lower legs, the step out of your skin clothes, your soft feet tapping all around the soft legs emptying the soft sounds of babies crying what about the lovers lying down in a pile on the ground when the police come with the headlights on?

2. guy starts—to bulge turn into horse creature—woman has flashback of her father asking her to carve the grid in his back.
when they kissed their mouths were moving tongues dancing. cold moisture in the air made the sand stick to the flesh above their knees, especially the flesh wet from licking. the land below her heart was splashed by the ocean and she had to remove her clothes. son, what are you drinking there with your shorts pulled down? and what's that little girl got between her fingers?

3. cops leave, horse creature born, named Poof.
oh god the gross feelings of squirting alive cutting the flesh around where it hurts better than keeping to have the pain—why are you turning so big help me—cut me so I can come alive the dancing the horse needs to be dancing—an incision around the edges of his thighs, around and underneath his scrotum and penis. the night air was cold and the wind brought a peaceful sound against the crashing waves which hit the rocks hard and made a ripping sound as they went back into the ocean to form again as another something in the water. in the distance dolphins and gulls could be heard splashing and pressing through ocean water.

4. with Poof go and decide to find homeless men and take them to their house and feed them cakes filled with random medication, convincing them that it is their birthday   when they take the cake, male or female, they are all named Joe.

as his body shrank and the area that had been his pelvis and thighs blossomed into a membrane, Elaine thought about the cutting that had last happened to her. she was seven he said she cried too much, then he had stopped and moved away from her where she had been lying on her bed. he went and sat in a chair and stared at her for a long time she cried then father took out a knife he told her to make a pattern of five horizontal and five vertical lines on his back with the knife. somehow that had never come up again.

5. when the bodies eat enough cake they fall into vegetative state and start to swell up. they start storing the bodies in a big dark room.
so we were walking to the store and daddy says let's go and see what's in the trash dumpster today? and they go and look and find a bum type's body and they put him in the shopping cart and carry him home. they shot him with a hypodermic needle so he was doubly unconscious. they scratched the marks into his back and took him back to the dumpster.

6. when she finds swelling on her body she decides she better tell her mother that her father molested her before she also enters this swollen, vegetative state where the bodies take on a grey complexion. she takes Poof with her.
when he woke up they had made him a cake and hit him with a paperweight so that he would start going by a different name. one time they brought back a woman. they called the person, man or woman, Joe.

7. the mother knew. they go down to the beach. Poof trots with the waves, running. the mother says was always too scared to do anything about the situation. they embrace, but awkwardly, because the daughter's body has begun to swell and hurt so they have to be careful.
they had a big house with many rooms. they didn't know what was in all the different rooms. they would push a cart around and put different kinds of pills in each cake. so they had people baking for them all the time. the house always smelled of good things to eat.

Lovely Language I Have Heard

COMPILED BY EVAN CANTOR

12/16/93	"fuck" "fuckin'" "this shithole" "Jackassville" "sleaze over to..."
12/17/93	"I feel like hell" "those fuckers" "kabosh on this shit"
12/20/93	"completely fuckin' crazy" "goddamn" "idiot morons"
1/7/94	"fuckin' happy to be here" "drag my ass" "dull out my desk" "oh shit!" "dammit"
1/10/94	"that scumhole" "fucking great" "that little fucker" "somethin' fuckin' funny"
1/11/94	"who the hell" "damn!"
1/12/94	"bullshit" "get off my ass" "dial up that crap" "oh shit" "like hell"
1/13/94	"that fuckin' thing" "eyeball the goodies"
1/20/94	"pull the plug and flush her right down the toilet" "shit that *has* shit" "looks like they vomited on them" "the hell-hole" "sit there picking your little nose"
1/21/94	"I don't give a damn"
1/24/94	"I'm going to shoot myself" "what could happen? I could get shot in the back" "fuck, fuck, fuck" "no shit!" "fuck up the program" "sucky" "damn, damn, damn, damn, damn"
1/26/94	"she's a fucking nightmare" "I think I have a tapeworm" "snowing like a booger"

1/27/94	"eyeball the little booger" "I'm going to kill myself" "if I farted around long enough" "more shit than we can deal with" "all this heavy shit" "all that crap"
1/28/94	"ten tons of crap" "fuckin'" "what the fuck" "throw myself on the floor and have a stroke"
1/31/94	"I felt like I was gonna shit in my pants" "rats, rats, rats, rats, rats" "shit! damn, damn, damn, damn, damn" "screw *this* shit" "they charge me up the butt for mine"
2/1/94	"my birthstone stinks"
2/3/94	"a bunch of shit" "shit everywhere" "more shit than I can deal with" "all this shit"
2/4/94	"it was a bitch"

Contributors' Notes

BAYARD JOHNSON

Francois Coover submitted 49 short stories per year for the last 11 years to various journals without a single acceptance. Eighteen months ago Francis Coover (no relation) became an assistant editor at the *Kenyon Review*. Since Francis Coover was listed on the masthead of the *Kenyon Review*, Francois Coover has had short stories published by *The Paris Review*, *The Southern Review*, *Housewife-Writer's Forum*, *Triquarterly*, *Tales of the Heart* and *Chariton Review*.

Shoshana Camoin's first published novel is *Death Becomes Them* (Cliffhanger Press), the story of a writer who murders the editors-in-chief of literary journals who reject her manuscripts. This novel has nothing to do with recent staff deaths at *Northwest Review*, *Heresies* and *Salt Lick Press*; any resemblance to persons living or dead is purely coincidental.

Jonathan Brown is able and willing to completely suppress his gag reflex in order to get his fiction published (just as we had to completely suppress our gag reflex in order to publish it). "Please Please Please I'll Do Anything Plus 2 More Inches" is his first published story.

Lydia Friedman has faithfully subscribed to this magazine since its inception and never fails to submit several entries to our annual "Suicide, Death, and Thighs" Poetry Contest, our biannual "Short Short Short Short Short Story in One Paragraph or Less" short fiction contest, our "Not Necessarily Read" annual novel competition, and our monthly "A. O. Burmeister Oratory Award" contest, each entry accompanied by her **nonrefundable** $20.00 money order **per entry** (no checks please). Our vacation schedule has made it inconvenient for the editors to find the time to read her "Mungo Park Bites Baaaack," included in this issue, but we hope you will have time to read it.

Gore Vidal and **William Buckley** are identical twins that were separated at birth.

B. H. Abeles is a pseudonym for the son of the editor-in-chief of this publication. Abeles desperately needs a publishing credit in order to keep from being fired from his/her faculty position teaching creative writing at the Point Barrow campus of the University of Alaska.

James Dixon is a pseudonym for the father of B. H. Abeles and has been anthologized in every one of our contest issues since this magazine's inception. His work-in-progress "Never Been Better" is not included in this issue, though the title appears in its entirety in the table of contents.

Kim Davidson's autobiographical memoir *Daddy's Wet Dream*, excerpted in this issue, is based on the autobiographical haiku song cycle written by B. H. Abeles about his/her father.

R. Hall has published a poetry chapbook, *Chaps Ink.* (published simultaneously by City Lights and Gay Sunshine Press) that deals with cowboy clothing motifs in the San Francisco tattoo culture. "Hotpoint Rangerover" is her first published poem that doesn't include the word "chaps."

Bayard Johnson declined to list any biographical information.

Boots, whose artwork graces our cover, is a hamster and recipient of a 1994 NEA/Santa Monica Arts Council "Art in the Parks" grant.

Kime Smegma is the first man ever to have breast implants (38-D) for the sole purpose of having people talk about her. "Women Dig It, No Shit" is the exact same story that has appeared in *Northwest Review, Friction,* and *Epiphany,* each time under a different title. Kime has just won the Ron Howard Creative Writing/Teaching Fellowship and will enroll in the UCLA Graduate Film School Program in the Fall.

Richard "Speck" Bartkowech lives in L.A., just bought a gun and is about to come unglued. "Die, Fucker" is his first published essay.

James Daniel claims his real name is Richard Brautigan and feels exonerated by the CIA murder of the imposter known to the world as Richard Brautigan.

Larry Davis has translated numerous ancient Gaelic poems into English in spite of having no previous knowledge of the Gaelic language.

Max Factor composes in lipstick and nailpolish and is the official Portrait Laureate for First Ladies Ford, Reagan, Bush, Clinton and Merrilee Rush.

Hans Oates is editor of the *Peninsular Review* at Cal State, Chino. "Bite" is his second story to appear in this publication. In the last 18 months the *Peninsular Review* has published fiction and poetry by an impressive 71% of this publication's editorial staff.

Phil Spector denies having been responsible for fucking up more good rock and roll than any other human in history, living or dead, with the possible exception of the New Christie Minstrels.

Andy Warhole is the stage name of Robert Dole, seen here modeling fashions by Victoria's Secret.

Albert Einstein is the author of *Uh...What?*, *Then Again, Er, Maybe Not* and *But, Well, It Seemed to Make Sense at the Time*.

Georges Pompidou and his...